Also Known as Elvis

Other Books by James Howe

Misfits Novels
The Misfits
Totally Joe
Addie on the Inside

Other Novels
A Night Without Stars
Morgan's Zoo
The Watcher

Edited by James Howe
The Color of Absence: Twelve Stories About Loss and Hope
13: Thirteen Stories That Capture the Agony and Ecstasy of Being Thirteen

Sebastian Barth Mysteries
What Eric Knew
Stage Fright
Eat your Poison, Dear
Dew Drop Dead

Bunnicula Books
Bunnicula (with Deborah Howe)
Howliday Inn
The Celery Stalks at Midnight
Nighty-Nightmare
Return to Howliday Inn
Bunnicula Strikes Again!
Bunnicula Meets Edgar Allan Crow

Tales from the House of Bunnicula
It Came from Beneath the Bed!
Invasion of the Mind Swappers from Asteroid 6!

Howie Monroe and the Doghouse of Doom
Screaming Mummies of the Pharaoh's Tomb II
Bud Barkin, Private Eye
The ~~Amazing~~ Odorous Adventures of Stinky Dog

Bunnicula and Friends
The Vampire Bunny
Hot Fudge
Rabbit-cadabra!
Scared Silly
Creepy-Crawly Birthday
The Fright Before Christmas

Pinky and Rex Series
Pinky and Rex
Pinky and Rex Get Married
Pinky and Rex and the Mean Old Witch
Pinky and Rex and the Spelling Bee
Pinky and Rex Go to Camp
Pinky and Rex and the New Baby
Pinky and Rex and the Double-Dad Weekend
Pinky and Rex and the Bully
Pinky and Rex and the New Neighbors
Pinky and Rex and the Perfect Pumpkin
Pinky and Rex and the School Play
Pinky and Rex and the Just-Right Pet

Picture Books
There's a Monster Under My Bed
There's a Dragon in My Sleeping Bag
Teddy Bear's Scrapbook (with Deborah Howe)
Kaddish for Grandpa in Jesus' name amen
Horace and Morris but mostly Dolores
Horace and Morris Join the Chorus (but what about Dolores?)
Horace and Morris Say Cheese (which makes Dolores sneeze!)

Also Known as Elvis

JAMES HOWE

Atheneum Books for Young Readers
New York   London   Toronto   Sydney   New Delhi

ATHENEUM BOOKS FOR YOUNG READERS
An imprint of Simon & Schuster Children's Publishing Division
1230 Avenue of the Americas, New York, New York 10020
This book is a work of fiction. Any references to historical events, real people, or real places are used fictitiously. Other names, characters, places, and events are products of the author's imagination, and any resemblance to actual events or places or persons, living or dead, is entirely coincidental.
Text copyright © 2014 by James Howe
Cover photograph copyright © 2014 by Michael Frost
All rights reserved, including the right of reproduction in whole or in part in any form.
ATHENEUM BOOKS FOR YOUNG READERS is a registered trademark of Simon & Schuster, Inc.
Atheneum logo is a trademark of Simon & Schuster, Inc.
For information about special discounts for bulk purchases, please contact Simon & Schuster Special Sales at 1-866-506-1949 or business@simonandschuster.com.
The Simon & Schuster Speakers Bureau can bring authors to your live event. For more information or to book an event, contact the Simon & Schuster Speakers Bureau at 1-866-248-3049 or visit our website at www.simonspeakers.com.
Also available in an Atheneum Books for Young Readers hardcover edition
Interior design by Mike Rosamilia, cover design by Russell Gordon
The text for this book is set in Avenir LT.
Manufactured in the United States of America
0315 OFF
First Atheneum Books for Young Readers paperback edition April 2015
2 4 6 8 10 9 7 5 3 1
The Library of Congress has cataloged the hardcover edition as follows:
Howe, James, 1946–
Also known as Elvis / James Howe. — 1st ed.
p. cm.
Summary: While his friends Bobby, Joe, and Addie are spending the summer on exciting adventures, thirteen-year-old Skeezie Tookis must get a job and help around the house, and things only get worse when his long-lost father appears.
ISBN 978-1-4424-4510-9 (hc)
ISBN 978-1-4424-4511-6 (pbk)
ISBN 978-1-4424-4512-3 (eBook)
[1. Single-parent families—Fiction. 2. Summer employment—Fiction.
3. Fathers and sons—Fiction. 4. Mothers and sons—Fiction.
5. Family life—Fiction. 6. Friendship—Fiction.] I. Title.
PZ7.H83727Als 2014
[Fic]—dc23
2013015974

For my brother Doug

Twelve years later . . .

Dear Little E,

Okay, so your name is going to be Elvis. But since your mom calls *me* Elvis (which is not my real name), I hope you don't mind if for now I call you Little E.

Man, how did I get to be twenty-five and having a kid? It's crazy! It seems like yesterday that I was hanging out at the Candy Kitchen and got called Elvis for the first time because of my slicked-back hair and black leather jacket.

The Candy Kitchen is this soda fountain and sandwich kind of place that's been around forever in our little town of Paintbrush Falls. My parents went there. My grandparents went there. And my best friends, Bobby, Addie, Joe, and I went there. Over the years, the only thing that changed was, they took out the jukebox. Otherwise, it was like a time capsule. And eventually they brought back the jukebox. Or I did. But hey, I'm getting ahead of myself.

And anyway, maybe you know all this already. I

don't know how much you can hear in there. By the time you're born and old enough to read this, you'll know a lot of it. But I still need to tell you, because it's the story of the summer that changed my life. I keep thinking that if things had worked out differently, I wouldn't be here today and you wouldn't be here in three weeks and six days. (That's when you're supposed to be born. If you're like me, you'll show up when you feel like it.)

The story begins twelve years ago, the end of June. Bobby, Joe, Addie, and I were hanging out at the Candy Kitchen, where we always hung out, in the last booth on the right with the torn red leatherette upholstery. We were having a Forum, which is what Addie called it when we talked about "Important Stuff." Addie wrote down every word, like we were the United Nations or something.

Oh, and just so you know, your mom is the only one who calls me Elvis anymore. To everybody else, I'm Skeezie.

Like I said, it was the end of June, the summer between seventh and eighth grade.

FORUM: "What I'll Be Doing on My Summer Vacation"

Skeezie: If the service gets any slower in here . . .

Addie: Relax, Skeezie. It's summer.

Skeezie: Meaning?

Addie: Meaning, it's okay for things to move slower.

Joe: Besides, in case you haven't noticed, HellomynameisSteffi is the only waitperson working today.

Skeezie: "Waitperson"? Really?

Addie: It's the nonsexist term.

Skeezie: Well, this "eat person" is hungry and can't wait anymore.

Addie: Skeezie! <u>Please</u> stop snapping your fingers!

Bobby: Change of subject. Can you believe seventh grade is actually over? Now all we have to do is survive eighth grade.

Joe: And high school.

also known as elvis

Skeezie: And life. Oh, good, here she is. Hey, Steff.

Hellomy nameis Steffi: Hey yourself, Elvis. You snapped?

Skeezie: Yeah, I was thinking, should I try these new sweet potato fries you've got on the menu?

Hellomy nameis Steffi: I'm glad you're doing some deep thinking, Elvis. Why don't you keep it up and answer that question for yourself?

Skeezie: In the words of the King, don't be cruel.

Hellomy nameis Steffi: I'm sure a lot of people other than Elvis Presley have said that, but in the interests of my other customers, I'll cut the cruelty and say, Yes, Big E, try the sweet potato fries. They are awesome.

Skeezie: Sold! And Dr Peppers all around!

Bobby: With a scoop of vanilla ice cream in
         mine, please.

Joe: And mine.

Addie: How is it that you're the only one
         working today, Steffi?

Hellomy
nameis
Steffi: We lost two employees. Adam's going
         to college in the fall and is biking
         across the country this summer.

Bobby: Cool!

Hellomy
nameis
Steffi: Right? And Tina got a better job at that
         new frozen yogurt place at the mall.
         Listen, I'd love to keep chatting, but
         before <u>other</u> people start snapping
         <u>their</u> fingers . . .

Skeezie: Yeah, yeah.

Hellomy
nameis
Steffi: Be right back.

Addie:	That is so cute. She called you "Big E."
Joe:	I don't get it. You don't have big ears.
Bobby:	Or elbows.
Joe:	Yeah, your elbows seem pretty normal to me. Although I have noticed that your eyeballs pertude.
Addie:	Protrude.
Joe:	Whatever.
Skeezie:	One, my eyeballs do not protrude. Two, it was not cute. And three, can we move on from the subject of HellomynameisSteffi? And four, if I owned this place, the "waitpeople" would not have to wear those dumb hellomynameis badges.
Addie:	Whatever you say, Big E. So today's topic is—
Bobby:	Addie! School's over. Can't we just hang out for once and not talk about Important Stuff?
Addie:	All I was going to say is, today's topic is "What I'll Be Doing on my Summer

Vacation." I'll start. <u>I</u> am going to
volunteer at the public library!

Skeezie: Wait. That sound you just heard was my
           brain going to sleep.

Addie: Just because you've never read a book
           in your life.

Skeezie: That's not true. I read your copy of
           <u>From the Mixed-Up Files of Mrs. Basil
           E. Somebody</u> back in the fourth grade.

Addie: It's "Frankweiler"—and <u>that's</u> where it
           went! May I have it back, please?

Skeezie: Um, I'm not quite finished with it. I
           think I have, like, a hundred pages left.

Addie: If I weren't using my hands to write
           this down, I would throttle you. Oh,
           and next month I'm going to stay
           with my grandma for a week, and
           then in August my parents and I are
           taking a two-week road trip. New
           York, Philadelphia, Baltimore, and
           Washington, DC!

Joe: Ooh, will you bring me something from

	Broadway? T-shirt, snow globe, cute chorus boy . . .
Skeezie:	You are so gay.
Joe:	You are so not and should only be so lucky. So, do you want to hear what I'm doing this summer? Well, Kelsey and me. We're going to be art counselors at the day camp.
Bobby:	Kelsey didn't tell me you were doing that with her. You'll be really good at it.
Joe:	Thanks. And then my family's going to Montreal for a week, where I will parlez-vous français and change my name to Jacques. Oh . . . oh . . . oh! And I forgot. Addie, you don't have to get me any of that stuff from Broadway, because— drumroll, please—I am going by myself (with a little help from the fabulous Trailways bus system) to visit Aunt Pam in the Big Apple. What about you, Bobby?
Bobby:	Well, since I'm no longer working at Awkworth & Ames . . .

Skeezie: Department Store of the Living Dead.

Bobby: Um, yes, it is kind of quiet.

Addie: I heard it might close. I hate that. I know it's kind of an anachronism and nobody ever shops there, but it's just such a part of Paintbrush Falls. I can't imagine it not being here.

Joe: A what-ism?

Addie: Anachronism. That's something that doesn't fit the time period it's in, like it belongs in an earlier time.

Joe: Oh. Like Skeezie.

Addie: Precisely.

Skeezie: Sound of me laughing. Not.

Addie: Anyway, the point is that sometimes change is hard.

Bobby: I know what you mean. But I like my new job so much better. I'm working with my dad out at the nursery.

Skeezie: The one near the Stewart's where my mom works?

Bobby: Uh-huh. I'll be outdoors working with

plants and all. Who knows, I might
even lose some weight. And it's really
good for my dad and me to have the
time together. At the end of July we're
going on a camping trip to Indian Lake
for a week. We've never had a vacation
together, just the two of us. Never. So
what are you doing this summer, Skeezie?

Skeezie: Sleep. Maybe finish that book of
Addie's. Eat ice cream. Sleep.

Addie: Seriously.

Skeezie: I'm being serious.

Joe: Well, it's nice to know you have
ambitions, Skeeze.

Skeezie: Hey, our food!

Hellomy
nameis
Steffi: Here's your sweet potato fries, Big E.

Addie,
Joe, and
Bobby: Awwwww.

Skeezie: You guys. Shut. Up.

**Hellomy
nameis
Steffi:** So I was overhearing your conversation.
What <u>are</u> you doing this summer, Elvis?
Hanging out at the pool, driving the girls
crazy?

Skeezie: Not likely. Yeah, no, I've got plans, sort
of, I just . . . hey, these sweet potato
fries are <u>excellent</u>.

**Hellomy
nameis
Steffi:** I'm glad you like them.

Bobby: You look tired, Steffi. You should take a
break.

**Hellomy
nameis
Steffi:** No kidding. But as Elvis put it: Not
likely. Well, eat up, you guys. And give
me a yell—I mean, snap—if you need
anything.

The truth, Little E? The truth is, I didn't have a clue what I was going to do that summer, but I was pretty sure there were some things I *wasn't* likely to be doing:

1. go on vacation with my family
2. spend any time with my dad
3. have fun

My mom (your future grandma) had already told me that she needed me to help out even more than usual with my sisters because she'd taken on a second job, and she wanted me to get a job because my dad was behind in his payments and times were tough. How was I going to tell that to the gang? I mean, I could pretty much tell them anything, but when Bobby was sitting there going on about being best buds with his dad and everybody was talking about the fantastic vacations they were going to take with their families, well, I hope you can appreciate—as much as it's possible for anybody to appreciate anything before they've even been born—how hard it was for me to be honest.

And that's the other part of the truth: There were things I wasn't being honest about with my friends. I'd never let them know just how bad things had gotten at home. I'd stopped inviting them over. I didn't want them to see that I wasn't the same Skeezie at home as the Skeezie they knew and loved in the outside world. I didn't want them to see my mom and me go at it, which we were doing more and more.

Like that day, when I got home from the Candy Kitchen.

When Your Dad Leaves, Part of Your Mom Leaves, Too

So I get home after hanging out at the Candy Kitchen with my friends, and my mom is waiting, already furious at me, and I haven't even done anything yet.

"You were supposed to be home thirty-seven minutes ago," she goes.

"It's just five," I say.

"It's five thirty-seven. If you wore the watch I bought you, you would know that. And you would also know that I have to be at the store in twenty-three minutes. I needed to talk to you, Skeezie. You said you'd be back in time so we could talk. And I need your help with supper for the girls."

"I'll make supper for the girls, geez. Since when *don't* I make supper for the girls?" It's true. I could have my own reality show: *Underage Chef.*

"Fine. But we still need to talk." My mom is in

the bathroom off the kitchen while she says this, tossing back a couple of drugstore-brand aspirins and sighing after she closes the medicine cabinet and catches sight of her own tired face in the mirror. "God, I look old," she says. I have to agree, although I know enough not to say it out loud.

My mom used to look like the kind of mom your friends would meet and say they couldn't believe she was your mom. She used to be young and pretty. She used to look happy. Now she looks old, and if she is happy, I guess I don't know what that looks like anymore.

"So talk," I say.

"Right. In the two minutes I have before I have to leave. Okay, Mr. I Won't Wear a Watch . . ."

"Because you bought it at the dollar store and it broke."

"Whatever. In the two minutes we have together, here's what I have to say. You're not in school, we can't afford a vacation, and I need help because there's stuff around the house that needs fixing. I *need* you to get a job, Skeezie."

"I know. You've only told me, like, a hundred times. But I'm thirteen. What kind of job am I going to get? And besides, what about my *unpaid* job as full-time nanny to your snot-nosed daughters?"

"That's just helping out. And talk nice."

"Yeah, well, who's going to cater to Megan's every wish if you and me are both working all the time? Who's going to hear her snap her fingers?"

(I do not pause to consider that finger snapping may run in the family.)

My mom puts on her lipstick like it's the last thing she wants to do. "For god sakes, Skeezie. I'm talking about a *part-time* job to bring in a few extra dollars. You keep half, give half to me for the house. You want to keep listening to the back door banging every time we forget to latch it? You *like* having to use the plunger every other time we go to the john?"

"Okay, okay," I say, deciding not to point out the lipstick she just got on her teeth. "But there are child labor laws. You never heard of those?"

Now she begins to cry, and I immediately feel guilty about the lipstick, even though I had nothing to do with putting it there. "What about *mom* labor laws?" she chokes out. "I never knew that when I went into labor with you I'd never get out of it!"

"If Dad hadn't left . . . ," I start to say.

"Stop right there! If your dad hadn't left, we might have killed each other by now. It's a lose-lose, Skeezie, so let's not go down that road, okay? Let's just leave it. And now *I've* got to leave. Our two minutes of quality time is up. Please. Find something, anything, just help me out here. Talk to Bobby. *He* works to help *his* family out."

I hate it when she does that. Brings in my friends as role models. It's so stinkin' unfair.

She glances in the mirror, yanks a tissue off the top of the toilet tank from the crocheted box she made back in better times, and wipes the lipstick off her teeth. And what can I say, she looks so sad and even older than she did two minutes ago that I tell her, "Okay, Mom. I'll get a job. I'll help."

I feel older now, too.

The back door slams. And as soon as she hears the car start up in the driveway, Megan shouts from her bedroom, "What's for supper? I'm starving!"

I hate my dad so much I want to punch the wall. I look into the bathroom mirror, half expecting to see my mom still there, but what I see is my own skinny face with its most recent acne acquisitions and an expression I don't even recognize. I don't like the me that's looking back.

"Spaghetti!" I shout.

"*Again?*"

Jessie, who's five and not nine-going-on-twenty-five like Megan, appears out of nowhere, grabs me around my legs, and squeezes real hard. "I *love* spaghetti!" she says, like it's "I love you!" I wish my friends could see this moment of Jessie hugging my legs, but not what went before it. I don't want them to see that. I don't want them to see the me I just saw in the mirror.

Nails Sticking Out of the Walls Where My Dad Used to Be

My dad left a little over two years ago, when I was in the fifth grade. Megan was in the second grade and Jessie was just three. I guess you could say I saw it coming, but it's kind of like hurricane warnings. You think, "Yeah, the rain's getting kind of heavy, but a hurricane? Not going to happen here." And then it hits.

It had been raining pretty hard. By which I mean, they'd been fighting a lot. About my dad being a bum, because he wanted to spend more time on his Harley than with his family—or working, for that matter. And my mom wanting to go back and finish college so she could get a decent job, but she couldn't because we needed the money from whatever jobs she managed to get. She wanted to be a nurse, but what she's been doing for a few years now is work in a doctor's office, answering phones and fighting with insurance companies. And now she's got this second job out at Stewart's, which makes me really nervous because it's one of those places people pull into to fill up with gas and she's alone there at night sometimes. When I think of her working there, I think:

1. I hate my dad for leaving us and making my mom have to work there, and
2. I hate me for even thinking I shouldn't get a job and help her out.

Anyways, I don't guess my dad was ever cut out to be a dad, even though he could be fun sometimes, like out at the lake or running around the backyard. My mom took lots of pictures at times like those, which was totally crazy because those pictures made us look like one big, happy family. And my dad looked like one happy dude. Or dad. But when he left, he didn't take one picture with him. Not one picture to remember us by. And my mom took all the pictures that had him in them off the walls and left the nails sticking out. Nice, right? I'd get really mad at her about that and she'd say, "Don't displace your anger, Skeezie. It's your dad you're mad at, not me."

That was her therapy talking. Yeah, she went to see a therapist for a while after he left. So did I, for about ten minutes. It was all on account of my dad's leather jacket. But that's a whole other story. And anyways, I don't think I was displacing anything, I think I was mad at my mom for leaving those ugly nails there, making our wall look as torn up as our lives.

A lot of things changed after my dad left.

1. All of a sudden, I was the only guy in the house. We had a couple of goldfish, but they looked too pretty to be guys. Addie and Joe would call me a sexist for that one, but it doesn't matter whether they were guys or not, because they died about three days

later since nobody bothered to feed them.

2. Being the only guy, I had to put up with my mom saying, "You're the man of the family now, Skeezie." Which when you're ten years old is not something you want to hear.

3. The house became a pigsty. It was never the neatest house in the world, but my mom got so depressed she didn't have the energy to yell at us kids to pick up our stuff. She's not so depressed anymore, but now when she yells at us, I can tell that her heart really isn't in it.

4. The yard became a dump. Okay, that's an exaggeration. I still cut the grass and all, but my mom had these beautiful gardens in the front and around back that she loved. She let them go, and since nobody but her is a gardener around here, now we have weeds where there used to be roses.

5. Megan started acting tough, like she didn't care our dad had left. She'd call him bad names, which my mom would tell her not to do until Megan wore her down and then instead of saying, "Don't talk about your father that way," she'd go, "You got *that* right, girl!"

6. Jessie started crying a lot, including in her sleep, which she didn't remember doing even when Megan would say the next morning, "How am I supposed to get my beauty sleep when my dumb sister wakes me up with her dumb crying?" Mom and me, we'd tell her not to say that about her sister, but nobody addressed the question of a seven-year-old needing beauty sleep.

7. I started wearing my dad's leather jacket that he left hanging in the closet. I nabbed it right before my mom was going to toss it in the trash. She hated that I wore that jacket, and when I say

also known as elvis

I wore it, I mean I wore it *all the time*, didn't matter how hot it was or how ridiculous I might have looked. I still do. It's my jacket now. It's what I have left of my dad, other than a bunch of stupid nails sticking out of a stupid wall.

How I Find My Summer Job

The next morning I ride my bike out to Carlson's Nursery to talk to Bobby. Okay, really it's to see if I can get a job. But Bobby's my go-to guy for most everything, so I figure he's a good place to start.

When I get there, I spot him right away, watering the hanging baskets out front. It's funny, I never thought of Bobby as an outdoor kind of person, maybe because he's on the heavy side and doesn't look like he gets a lot of exercise. Or maybe it's because I'm not an outdoor kind of person myself, so I figure how could any of my best friends be. But there he is, getting tan after only a few days of working here and I swear already looking thinner. *And* he's going camping with his dad next month. *Camping.*

"Hey, Skeezie!" he calls out when he sees me. I drop my bike and follow after him as he goes to turn off the hose. "What are you doing out here? Isn't it hot in that jacket?"

"Kind of," I say. "So how's it going?"

"Great. Mrs. Carlson—Nancy—is really nice. I haven't even been here a week and she's taught me so much already. She says by the end of the summer I'll know enough to open my own nursery!"

"Is that what you want to do?"

Bobby laughs. "No, I want to go into the eighth grade and survive it. But maybe I can convince my dad to start his own business. And I could help out."

"That would be cool."

"A lot cooler than selling ties at Awkworth & Ames," he says, and I think he's got that right. Bobby's last job—and his boss, Mr. Kellerman—gave me the creeps.

Just then, his dad shows up pushing a wheelbarrow full of stinky-smelling dirt.

"Skeezie!" he shouts as if the dirt is a loud noise he needs to be heard over. I don't know about that, but it sure is making my eyes water.

"Hey, Mike," I go. "What's up with that dirt? It smells like, well . . ."

He laughs. "That's because that's what it is. It's fertilizer. So what brings you out here? I don't imagine you came all this way to smell this. Hey, you want to help out?"

I shrug. "Maybe," I say. "Kind of."

How do you ask for a job? I have no idea.

Bobby has been my friend for most of my life, so he's pretty good at reading my mind. "Are you looking for a summer job?" he asks.

I nod sheepishly, like his question is embarrassing, which it kind of is but I don't know why. "My mom says I have to," I tell him.

Mike says, "Your mom works harder than anybody I know. If she says you have to, she must really need the help. Stay here. I'll see what I can do."

And just like that, he leaves us with the wheelbarrow full of stinky dirt and goes off into the office.

Bobby turns to me with this big smile on his face. "Wouldn't it be awesome if we could work together this summer?"

"Totally," I say.

We bump fists and start talking about what it will be like working together and what we'll bring for lunch every day and how much money we'll make. And then Mike comes back, his head down, and breaks it to me that they told him they can't afford to hire anybody else right now.

"I'm sorry, Skeezie," he says.

"That's okay." I can see from his face that he wanted to give me better news. Mike, like Bobby, is a good guy. "Thanks for asking anyways."

He suggests I try the stores in town and I tell him I will, although we agree I should steer clear of Awkworth & Ames.

As I'm getting back on my bike, I hear Mike call Bobby "Skip" and Bobby call his dad "Hammer," their at-home nicknames for each other. I look back over my shoulder and see Mike throw his arm around Bobby's shoulders, and I think maybe it's not so bad I didn't get a job here. Bobby and Mike are the only family they've got, so they're real close. I'm not sure where I would fit in.

* * *

Three days go by, and I've gone to all the stores in town, but nobody's hiring. One good thing: Addie's dad told me this morning he'd pay me to mow their lawn, which is really nice of him, because I once heard him say that mowing the lawn is his favorite form of meditation.

Okay, that's just plain weird, but Addie's parents are not exactly what you'd call normal and Addie has inherited their genes, so what can I say? Weirdness abounds.

Anyways, the point is that it was really nice of him to offer and I said I'd do it, but I still need a job. A few bucks once a week from mowing a lawn isn't going to get the toilet fixed.

So after my third morning of trying to convince people they should hire a thirteen-year-old with greasy hair and no skills over an unemployed college graduate, I stop at the Candy Kitchen to lift my downhearted spirits with a frosty Dr P. I'm wishing I had enough cash for some of those sweet potato fries, but that's going to have to wait until after I've mowed Addie's lawn next week.

Steffi is wiping down the counter when I open the door so hard it knocks over an umbrella stand. If there were any customers in the place, they'd probably yell at me or something. But Steffi's the only one that I can see, and she doesn't even look up.

"Hey, Elvis," she goes.

"How did you know it was me?" I answer. "Am I the only one who knocks over this stinkin' umbrella stand? And what's up with an umbrella stand? I mean, who puts their umbrellas in umbrella stands? Who *has* umbrellas?"

Steffi stops wiping and looks up at me. "You have a lot to say on the subject of umbrellas," she says. "Are you that interested or do you just like the sound of the word?" She brushes a strand of hair off her forehead, and I get this funny feeling like I'm going to tip over or something.

Okay. Up to now, I am the only one of the Gang of Five—that's what Addie and Bobby and Joe and me call ourselves even though there are only four of us; it's kind of an inside joke—anyways, I'm the only one who doesn't have a girlfriend or something. Don't ask, it's like their hormones are on steroids, because all three of them have girlfriends or boyfriends. Or *had*. Joe broke up with his boyfriend Colin a while back, and Addie and her boyfriend DuShawn broke up a month ago. But Bobby and his girlfriend Kelsey are still going strong.

Where was I?

Oh yeah, right. Steffi. So I'm standing here looking at her in her tight LIFE IS GOOD T-shirt with her HELLO MY NAME IS STEFFI badge right over the word *good*, watching her brush this strand of hair off her forehead, and I suddenly think I'm going to tip over and crash into the door and knock down the umbrella stand all over again, and it's so weird because, I mean, what is that about? How come I'm staring at somebody brushing stupid hair off their face, mumbling, "How should I know why I'm talking about umbrellas?" and "Yeah, umbrella's a pretty cool word," and waiting for a big hand to come down out of the sky and stamp 100% IDIOT on my forehead? Luckily, Steffi rescues me with, "You look like the heat's getting to you, Big E. How about a Dr Pepper? On the house."

"Really?" I can't believe it. If Steffi treats me to a Dr P, I'll have *almost* enough money for an order of sweet potato fries.

"Can I get *half* an order of sweet potato fries?" I ask.

"I'll give you a whole order for the price of half if you share," she says.

"Is that allowed?" I ask, like I'm running for president and trying to avoid a scandal.

"I have an in with the cook," she tells me. "He happens to be the boss. He also happens to be my cousin."

"Cool," I say. I'm not sure what's cool about it, but it seems like the right thing to say.

Steffi gets me a Dr P and I straddle a stool, while she goes off to the kitchen and gets us our sweet potato fries. I'm thinkin' how whack it is that I'm thinking Steffi is cool, and, yeah, she looks pretty good, but *she's six years older than me*. And then I remember how Bobby once told me how he had this big crush on Joe's aunt Pam, who is in her twenties, for cryin' out loud. I guess hormones don't worry about stuff like if somebody's your friend's aunt or could have been your babysitter just a few years before.

When Steffi returns and slides the basket in front of me, I notice that it's, like, a supersize portion. I pull out the measly single I have stuffed in my jacket pocket, along with a handful of change.

"Keep your money," she says. "I'm taking a break and can have anything I want."

I'm not sure she's telling the truth, because while she's eating the fries she keeps doing stuff like cleaning the milk shake machine and refilling saltshakers. That doesn't look like a break to me, but I'm not about to argue with free fries.

While I watch her work I notice two things: the way she moves her body to the music that's playing, which is a very nice thing to notice, and how whiny the singer is, which is not.

"This music sucks," I say, by way of making conversation.

Steffi spins around, slaps the damp rag on the counter, and grabs the basket of fries. "That's it!" she says. "No more fries for you!"

"What? What'd I say?"

"*That* is Patsy Cline!"

"Yeah, so?" I motion for her to return the fries, which she says she'll do after I wipe the ketchup off my face. What is she all of a sudden, my mother?

"Patsy Cline was one of the greatest country singers of all time," she informs me, putting the basket down about a foot away from where it had been before, in case she needs to grab it away in a hurry again, I guess. "Maybe the greatest. She's classic, like Elvis. And this song? This song is a classic."

"Doesn't mean I have to like it," I tell her.

Now she grabs a squeeze bottle of ketchup and holds it up to her lips like a mike. "'Crazy,'" she starts singing along, "'crazy for loving you.'"

Man. No matter where you turn, it's all about

love. Even the King, that's what he sings about, except in my two favorites, "Hound Dog" and "Blue Suede Shoes." Maybe that's why they're my favorites.

Steffi's singing gives me a chance to move the basket of fries closer and scarf down half my half. I've drained my Dr P by now, wishing I hadn't because the salt is getting to me. The song is starting to get to me, too, in a nice way, not because I like Patsy Whiny's voice any better, but because of the way Steffi sings. She's got her eyes closed and she's feeling it.

"You got a good voice," I tell her when the song ends and Patsy starts singing another one, something about falling to pieces or something.

"Thanks, Elvis," she says, looking serious and kind of sad. "You like to sing?"

I give her half a nod. I sing all the time in the shower and sometimes for my friends, but they tell me to shut up because they're tired of hearing "Hound Dog" and "Blue Suede Shoes," so I stick mostly to the shower.

Steffi gives me another Dr P without my even asking for it. She picks up a fry, sticks it in her mouth, and says, "The fries are getting cold." We both crack up at that, because that's supposed to be my line.

"So what's going on, Elvis?" she asks. "You're usually in here with your friends. Why the solo act today?"

I tell her about how I have to get a job and I'm having no luck. I think she's going to say, what do I expect, I'm only thirteen; I'm lucky to have somebody's grass to cut; I should be hanging out at the pool, driving the girls crazy. But she doesn't say any of those things.

Instead, she says, "I've been working since I was your age. Babysitting jobs first, which I still do, then helping out my mom in her shop, and then here for the past couple of years. We needed the money as far back as I can remember, and after my dad left, it was all hands on deck. Even my brother, who's pretty limited in what he can do, he's had to help out, too."

Maybe if I were older or smarter, I'd ask her about her brother 'cause it sounds like something's wrong with him, but all I can focus on right now is that her dad left her, like mine left me. I want to say something about that, but I don't have a clue what it should be. So I just say, "So you know what it's like."

"Yep," she goes. She leans on her elbows and looks me right in the eyes. This should make me extremely nervous, but for some reason it doesn't. I feel like I know what she's going to say next and I can't believe my luck. If luck is what it is.

"Why don't you work here this summer?" she asks me. I was right! "We can really use the help. I'll speak to my cousin Donny, but I know he'll say it's okay. You'll have to talk to him anyway about hours and pay and all that good stuff, but what do you think? All the fries you can eat. Not a bad deal, right?"

Not a bad deal at all. All the fries I can eat. Free Dr P's. And Steffi to look at. If we could just do something about the music, it would be perfect.

"I'll take it," I tell her.

"Great," she says.

We eat the rest of the fries before they get too cold, bopping our heads to Patsy Whiny. When she sings the words, "'I don't know what's comin' tomorrow; maybe it's trouble and sorrow,'" I think, *Like the T-shirt says, life is good.*

Turns out the T-shirt's wrong, and it's Patsy who's got it right.

Look What the Cat Dragged In

My mom's mom, Grandma Roseanne, doesn't talk a whole lot, and when she does she says things like, "My hip is killing me," or, "Feels like rain" (even when the sun is shining), or "Look what the cat dragged in." She's not exactly what you'd call full of good cheer.

Anyways, every time we go to visit, I walk in the door and she says, "Look what the cat dragged in." I never really got it. She lives with my aunt Lindsay and her family and, okay, they've got cats—five of them, to be exact—but not one of them has ever dragged me anywhere. Then one day one of them *did* drag something in. Half a dead mouse. That's when I understood what the expression means. "Look who I'm as happy to see as half a dead mouse." At least, that's what it sounds like every time my grandma says it.

Thanks, Grandma. I'm happy to see you, too.

also known as elvis

I think of this expression every time the door of the Candy Kitchen opens and somebody I know walks in. It's not like I think of my friends as half a dead mouse, it's just that the words are in my head. I never say them out loud, but every time Joe or Bobby or Addie or even my mom walks in the door, there I am thinking the cat dragged them in.

"Hey, Skeeze!"

I look up and there's Joe slamming open the door, just missing the umbrella stand, arm in arm with Zachary, his new best friend. The two of them are wearing bright-colored high-tops, baggy shorts, and these crazy Hawaiian shirts Joe would describe as "retro meets fashion forward" that they got at the thrift shop down by the Trailways station. It's like a two-person tween gay pride parade right here in Paintbrush Falls, except for the fact that Zachary isn't gay, or doesn't know yet that he is. I've got to hand it to Joe; he's got chutzpah. (That's a word I learned from Joe's grandmother, who has a lot more to say than mine, and half the time it's in this Jewish language called Yiddish. *Chutzpah* means nerve.)

Right behind them come Addie and *her* new bff, Becca. Well, okay, Becca isn't exactly her *best* friend. In fact, up until the end of the school year, they were more like frenemies, but then they started hanging out together and Becca lost some of her attitude and most of her makeup and turned out to be a whole lot nicer than anybody thought she was.

And, without all the makeup, a whole lot prettier.

By which I mean, she definitely does *not* make me think of half a dead mouse.

They surprise me by sitting at the counter instead of our booth at the back. I guess it's because that's where I am, putting away glasses that just came out of the dishwasher.

"So how are you guys?" I ask.

"Okay," Addie answers. "It was a slow day at the library."

This makes me laugh. "Um, is there ever a *fast* day at the library?"

"I just mean," says Addie, getting a little huffy,

"that there was hardly anyone there, even for story time. Does no one read *books* anymore?"

Becca says, "Books, books. I think I remember those. Weren't they those things made out of paper that had words in them?"

"Very funny," says Addie.

Joe says, "Well, consider yourself lucky that you weren't doing *my* job today, Addie. We were having the kids make these paper-bag wind socks, and this one boy, Jeremiah, who I swear is the devil's child, kept blowing up the paper bags and popping them in everyone's ears. And this girl, Eloise, who is very sensitive, wouldn't stop crying and saying that Jeremiah had made her deaf. And then this other boy, Liam, started screaming at Eloise because he thought she couldn't hear, and then this girl, Leeann, wet her pants."

Zachary starts laughing his goofy laugh, which makes everybody else laugh, and Addie says, "Okay, you win."

I love my friends. Seriously.

"And how's it going with you, E.B.?" Joe asks.

"Say what?" says Becca.

"E.B. Earring brother. Skeezie and I got our ears pierced together last Christmas, and we call ourselves earring brothers."

"Oh-kaaaay," Becca goes, like that's just about the uncoolest thing she's ever heard.

"I guess you had to be there," I say to Becca.

"I guess," she says. "But Skeezie, really, you could do better than that skull-and-crossbones thing. I mean, it's so trailer trash."

"Ouch," I say, and then Addie lets Becca have it for using that expression when all kinds of nice people live in mobile homes, including Bobby and his dad.

"Okay, okay, excuse me for living," says Becca. "I didn't know Bobby lived in a trailer."

"Even if he didn't, there are lots of people who do, and they are *not* trash," Addie goes on in this high-and-mighty tone, sounding like, well, Addie.

"Anyway," Becca says to me, "I didn't mean that *you* look like trailer trash, Skeezie. Just the earring. In fact, I think this job has, like, improved your appearance."

I wasn't aware that my appearance needed improvement. Apparently, that is a minority view.

"It's true," Addie says, while Joe and Zachary nod. The traitors. "Maybe it's just that you're out of that leather jacket for a change and are required by law to wash your hands, but you look more . . . I don't know . . . wholesome."

"Wow, the ultimate compliment," I go. "Just slap me between two slices of white bread, lay on the mayo, and have me for lunch."

This makes Becca laugh, and I notice that she has dimples.

And she notices that my face goes red.

"I'll have an ice cream sundae, with a cherry on top—just that color," she says, pointing to my cheeks.

Fortunately, this guy in one of the booths snaps his fingers and calls out for a check.

"Yeah, yeah," I tell him, but not so he can hear. "Don't get your panty hose in a twist."

"So how does it feel when somebody else is doing the finger snapping?" Addie asks.

I'm all set to give her a wise-guy answer (wise-guy answers are kind of my trademark) when Steffi comes over to write up the guy's check and asks me to refill some water glasses at another booth.

"You're kind of adorable when you're being efficient," Becca tells me as I grab the water pitcher. I feel my face go even redder as Steffi stifles a laugh.

After they're gone, Steffi says, "That girl with Addie—what's her name, Becky?"

"Becca."

"Becca. She likes you, Elvis."

"Right. A girl like Becca doesn't even *look* at a guy like me. Besides, who says I like *her*?"

"Nobody. But it's pretty obvious she likes *you*."

Trust me when I tell you that there is no way Becca Wrightsman likes me. Up until a few weeks ago, she barely acknowledged my existence, and when she did it was to make some put-down disguised as an observation. Like, "I can't decide which is older: that jacket you're always wearing or the food stuck in the corners of your mouth." This is *not* the kind of thing said by somebody who likes somebody.

It is, however, the kind of thing I was used to hearing. My friends and I, we got called all kinds of names all through elementary school and into middle school. Some of that changed after we ran for student council this year as the No-Name Party. We lost the election, but we got the school to start this thing called No-Name Day, and next year Mr. Kiley (that's the principal) said he's going to make it No-Name Week. Anyways, it's not like nobody ever calls anybody a name anymore, but at least people think about it. Or most people do.

"Hey, look who's the soda *jerk*!"

That? That's what the cat just dragged in. His name is Kevin Hennessey, and I don't think he thinks about anything, least of all the names he calls people. It's a couple of days later, and Kevin's walking in the door of the Candy Kitchen with his sidekick, Jimmy Lemon. Kevin doesn't go to our school anymore, so I haven't seen him in a long time. It's still not long enough.

"Perfect job for a *dago* like you," says Kevin with a snort. "You can grease up your hair in the deep fryer anytime you want."

Jimmy Lemon, who isn't much for snappy dialogue, mostly lets Kevin get in the good lines and then just repeats part of them like, "Yeah, deep fryer. Good one."

Before I can say anything, Donny, who happens to be up front at the moment, working the candy case, calls out, "Hey, none of that kind of talk in here. I'm Italian, my friend, and I'm going to ask you nicely to curb your language."

"I wasn't talking to you," Kevin goes. "And I'm not your friend."

"Okay," says Donny, "we got that established. Now I'm telling you—not asking nicely anymore—that if I hear that kind of talk from you again, you're out of here, and you won't be welcomed back."

Kevin rolls his eyes and gives a kind of *yeah, yeah* look with his face while secretly flipping Donny the bird. It looks like spending most of seventh grade in Catholic school didn't do a whole lot for Kevin's manners.

"So, *Squeezie*," Kevin says, throwing a leg over one of the stools at the counter like he's a cowboy and this is some Wild West saloon, "how about jerkin' me a soda?" This gets Jimmy Lemon laughing so hard he starts spitting. The two of them are like a small-town version of that movie *Dumb and Dumber*, I swear.

Lucky for me, I've only got five minutes left to work. Steffi jumps in and says, "I'll make that soda. Why don't you leave early? You didn't get a full break today."

1. I took seven extra minutes on my break today.
2. I note that she doesn't call me Elvis in front of Kevin and Jimmy.
3. Steffi is awesome.

So it works out that I don't have to put up with any more of Kevin's crap that day, but I know he'll be back. He's like a bear that's figured out where the fish run through the shallow part of the river. Easy picking, and for Kevin that's half the fun.

On a Friday afternoon about three weeks into the job, I almost wish it *were* Kevin the cat dragged in. I'm restocking the cones—waffle, sugar, and wafer (also known as cake)—when my grandma Roseanne shows up with Megan and Jessie.

"Hi, Grandma," I greet her.

"Everything in this place is fattening," she greets me back.

"Oh, sorry," I say. "You must have been lookin' for Weight Watchers. That's down the street."

"Don't be sassy," she says with a hint of a smile. Despite herself, Grandma likes a good wisecrack.

It's not the usual thing to see Grandma with the girls. She complains that they wear her out, for one thing, and for another she stopped driving after Grandpa died and she moved in with Aunt Lindsay, so she doesn't get out much.

"We wanted to show Grandma where you worked," Jessie says in that bubbly way she has. (I'm thinking that she must not have inherited a single gene from Grandma.) "Aunt Lindsay picked us up from day camp, and she's going to meet us here later."

I wipe down the booth they slide into and ask, "So how was camp today?"

"It was all right," Megan says, in this flat tone as if she is *so* over day camp and why does she have to go.

"It was *more* than okay, Megan," Jessie bubbles. "It was the best! Oh, Skeezie, look at my nails!"

She shows me her fingernails, painted in alternating purple-with-yellow-stars and red-with-pink-hearts.

"Let me guess," I say. "Joe did them, right?"

"Uh-uh. Kelsey. But she painted Joe's to match mine."

"Figures."

"And guess what else?"

"Um, you took a field trip to the moon? You

built a cabin out of Popsicle sticks? You sang all the verses of 'Ninety-nine Bottles of Beer on the Wall'?"

"No, silly. I don't even know what that is. And anyway, we don't sing about *beer* in day camp. Are you done guessing?"

Grandma shoots me a look that says, *Be done guessing.*

"Yep," I say.

"We're going to make family trees out of branches and pinecones."

"That is so dumb," says Megan.

Jessie punches Megan on the arm. "It is *not*! And that is *not* nice!"

"Well, good luck with *this* family tree," says Megan. "Where are you going to put Daddy? May as well leave him on the ground with the rest of the pinecones."

Jessie's eyes start to well up with tears.

"Okay, who wants what?" I ask. "I can do cones, dishes, sundaes, sodas, shakes, you name it."

"Diet Coke," Grandma snaps like she's made

some kind of earth-shattering decision. "With lots of ice. Don't stint on the ice."

The girls order sundaes, which Grandma says are to be *kiddie* sundaes, but which I know to make regular and call them kiddie.

Anyways, it isn't Grandma and Megan and Jessie who make me wish Kevin had been the one the cat dragged in that day. It's who comes in later, while they are finishing up their sundaes and Diet Coke (Grandma asked for three refills and kept saying, "They're free, right?"). Grandma is digging through her purse while I get the check from Steffi and tell her not to expect a big tip. Or any tip.

I am standing next to the cash register with my back to the front door and Steffi is writing up the check, when I hear the door swing open and Grandma say, "Well, look what the cat dragged in."

I think it has to be a joke—or maybe Aunt Lindsay showing up—but then I hear Jessie squeal, "Daddy!"

I turn and, sure enough, my dad is standing there with a big smile on his face, looking like the happy pinecone who's just found his way back to the family tree. Except to me, he looks more like half a dead mouse.

Frosty Goodness Gets Stuck in My Throat

Jessie runs to him with her arms spread wide. He somehow manages to scoop her up in a big bear hug at the same moment he reaches out and snatches the check from Steffi's hand.

"I'll take care of that," he goes, giving her a wink.

Is he kidding? Dude's gone missing for two years and now he comes barging in like he's the hero in some movie! Who does he think he's fooling?

Not my grandma, that's for sure. Snapping her purse shut, she glares at him and says, "It's the least you can do, with all you owe. I'd call you a name, but I don't want to insult your mother."

My dad smiles his famous killer smile. "Roseanne," he says, "always a pleasure."

It's not that I haven't seen my dad in the past two years. I have, maybe three or four times. Okay, four. But each time it's been like a drive-by, so the recent pictures I have of him in my mind aren't so much pictures as blurs. And he's never shown up out of the blue before. He's always called first, and he's always wanted something.

I give him a good hard look, trying to figure out what he wants this time. The first thing I notice is that he's put on weight, most of it in his belly. I can't help wondering if he's upped his beer consumption. The second thing I notice, which really should have been the first thing because it's so freakin' weird, is that he's wearing a tie. If I told you that I'd seen my dad wear a tie even one other time in his life, I'd be exaggerating. Ties and black leather jackets don't exactly go together. And that's when I notice he's not wearing a black leather jacket. (The one I wear is some reject he left behind; he must own at least a half dozen, and he was *always* wearing one of them.) Instead, he's got on a button-down shirt with the sleeves rolled up to the elbow. I see he's added another tattoo, some kind of weird dragon thing, on his left forearm. But he's clean-shaven. No 'stache, no stubble.

"What'd you go and do?" I ask him. "Join a cult?"

Jessie is hanging off his arm like a baby chimp. He's been pretty much keeping his eyes on her, avoiding the arctic wind that's blowing his way from Megan and Grandma. At the sound of my voice, he turns to look at me for the first time.

"I heard you were workin' here," he tells me. "Good for you."

"*Somebody's* got to pay for things," I say, like it's me who's putting food on the table, when all I've done so far is help get the toilet fixed.

"Like I said: good for you. I'm impressed. You got a work ethic."

"That's *one* of us," I mumble. I know my attitude can only go so far before it gets me in trouble. Time to turn down the volume.

I don't know if he heard me or not, but he doesn't take the bait. "It's good to see you, Skeezie," he says evenly, like he's practiced the line in a mirror. "You doin' okay?"

I shrug.

Then Grandma asks the question I've been asking in my head. "What do you *want*, BJ?"

Swinging Jessie from baby chimp position to piggyback, he answers, "Do I have to want something? Other than seeing my own kids once in a while?"

"You could have been seeing them every day instead of once in a while," my grandma says, sliding out of the booth and dusting imaginary crumbs off her lap. "Girls, it's time for us to go."

"Awwww," Jessie whines. "But he just got here. Daddy, you're coming back to the house, right? You're going to stay, right? Does Mommy know you're here? Let's call her."

Keeping her distance, Megan says, "Shut up, Jessie. Mommy does *not* want to know her ex-husband is in town."

"Hey, *you* shut up," my dad snaps at Megan, his face flashing the same red mine does when I'm angry or embarrassed. "She already knows I'm in town. I called her a couple of days ago. And FYI,

Miss Know-It-All, I am not her ex-husband yet. We never got divorced."

"Yay!" Jessie cries, wrapping her arms hard around my dad's neck.

Steffi hands him the check and says, "That's not a very nice way to talk to your daughter."

"You calling me out?" he asks. "Oops, there goes *your* tip."

"Hey!" I say, but Steffi stops me with a firm hand on my arm.

"It's okay, E," she says. "I shouldn't have said that, but I really hate it when people talk like that. Especially when the people are parents and the ones they're talking to are their kids."

My dad hands her a bunch of singles, which he's counted out to be sure it's the exact amount of the check. "Well, when you have kids, you can talk to them however you want," he tells her. "And I'll talk to mine the way they deserve. Fair enough?"

His face gets redder as he shrugs Jessie off, with a "C'mon, Jess, you're choking me here."

Jessie's flip-flops slap the floor when she lands. She grabs for my dad's hand, which he quickly moves up to straighten his tie.

"So I'll be seeing you guys later," he says to all of us. "Allie said it'd be cool for me to come by after supper. We got some catching up to do."

"Why don't you do your catching up with your parole officer and leave us be?" Grandma Roseanne says. This makes my dad laugh.

"Sure can't say I've missed your nasty tongue, Roseanne. But when you land a good one, you land a good one. And that was a good one."

For the record, my dad does not have a parole officer. He's a bum, but he's not a criminal.

When he turns back at the door and shoots a smile at us, I realize it's a salesman's smile. And that's just what he's doing: selling the new, improved version of himself to his kids, two out of three of whom aren't buying.

After the door swings shut, it's like the whole place lets out its breath. I'm really glad there weren't any other customers when he showed up.

And now that he's gone, I feel my own face getting red. Steffi notices, too.

"Easy, Elvis," she says. "Why don't you take your break now? Want me to fix you a Dr Pepper float?"

I nod and, letting my own breath out, count to ten, the way she taught me to a couple of weeks ago when Kevin Hennessey pushed my buttons one time too many and I wanted to deck him.

A car honks out front, and Grandma announces, "That's Aunt Lindsay. Megan, Jessie, we're going."

I say goodbye, to which:

1. Grandma grunts.
2. Megan says, "Whatever." And,
3. Jessie runs over and hugs my legs.

After they go, it hits me what my dad said about my mom already knowing he was coming. *That's* why I'm so mad. She never told us. Not a word. But boy, has she been in a sucky mood for the past few days. Finding fault with everything I did (or didn't do), yelling at the girls, slamming things, going outside to smoke (even though she says she's quit), talking under her breath on the phone. I figured she was talking to her sister, who's the one person I could think of who makes her nervous enough to need a cigarette. Now I know it was my dad the whole time, and the whole time she kept it a secret.

Steffi carries my float over to the booth I normally share with the Gang of Five, and I slide in after it, slumping down and slurping up the frosty goodness through double straws, wondering for the first time if what my dad wants is the same thing Jessie wishes for: to come back home, to be a dad again.

And this is where the frosty goodness gets stuck in my throat and it starts to burn. I hate to admit it, but there's a part of me that wants that, too.

Time Warp Meets "Do I Know You"

My mom calls in sick to her job at Stewart's that night. She gets a girlfriend or somebody to cover for her. I'm like, "What do you mean, you're not going to work?" Like I'm the parent all of a sudden and she's the one cutting school so she can do something fun—although how seeing my dad ever made it into the category of "something fun" is more than I can figure out.

It is *so weird*. Because after being a total crab for the past two days, she's all of a sudden acting like that's exactly what's going on: like my dad coming over is going to be fun. She's got some pop star nobody's going to remember in twelve years blasting on the boom box (the music at our house sucks almost as much as at the Candy Kitchen) while she bustles around the house, stuffing dirty socks and smelly sweatshirts into plastic bags from the Grand Union and tossing them down the cellar steps, shoving old magazines under the couch, trying to wipe away the three thousand rings that have accumulated on the coffee table since she stopped barking at us about using coasters, and checking herself out in the bathroom mirror every five minutes, putting her hair up on top of her head, then letting it flop back down to her shoulders.

"Wash your face," she orders me for the first time in two years.

I look at her like she's got a screw loose, which she totally does, and more than one.

"Excuse me?" I say, but she's moved on to shouting at Megan, who's barricaded herself in the bedroom she shares with Jessie. Jessie, who makes a career out of pounding on the door for Megan to let her in, has been happily occupied for hours in the middle of the kitchen floor, chirping along to the so-called music and making some sort of homecoming present for our dad. I have no idea what it's supposed to be, but it involves about a thousand Popsicle sticks and at least two bottles of glue.

When I hear my mother yell at Megan to get

herself out here this minute and Megan yell back, "Make me!" I think maybe the fun times are over and I duck out the back door.

I head to my secret hideaway: the kennel where we kept the one dog we ever had. It looks like an abandoned prison, which it basically is, but in the back of it there's a wooden doghouse that's big enough for me to crawl into and hunch up. It's pretty much falling apart, so it kind of looks like whatever that is that Jessie's making our dad, but I like it anyway. I pretend to myself that it still smells like Penny in here, even though she's been gone for, like, six years, and I probably can't even remember what she actually smelled like.

What stinks about this being my secret hideaway is that it reminds me of my dad almost as much as Penny, because he's the reason we got a dog in the first place, and he's the one who built the doghouse. But he's not the reason we stopped having her. Her being gone is one of the few things I can't blame on him, as much as I wish I could. But I don't like to think about that.

It's really hot in here, being July and all, so I take off my leather jacket and roll it up into a ball to put under my head. Lying back, I get to thinking about Penny, which makes me sad, and I can't help wishing that she was the one who found her way back home and not my dad. Yeah, I know she's never coming back. I mean, dogs don't come back after six years, even in the movies. I'm not that stupid.

This gets me thinking about when Becca was in the Candy Kitchen the other day and told me she might be getting a dog. "No fair," I'd said, like I was Jessie's age, and Becca had said, "'No fair'? Really?" like she thought I was Jessie's age, too.

I act like I don't care about girls, but the truth is I don't know how to talk around them. Other than Addie, who's not really a girl.

(Okay, dude, she's a girl. I get that. But she's not a girl like *that*. Not to me, anyways.)

Thinking about dogs and girls is getting weirdly mixed up in my brain, so it's probably a good thing that Jessie pops her head into the doghouse (my secret hideaway isn't that secret) and shouts, "Daddy's here!" like I'm not two feet in front of her.

"Big whoop," I answer, which makes her look like I just popped bubblegum all over her face, so I quickly add, "I'll bet he liked the present you made him."

"He thought it was supposed to be a bird-house," she tells me as she grabs my hand and pulls me up, "when it is *obviously* a pencil holder, but that's okay, because he said he liked it, and I told him I put a *lot* of work into it, and he told me it showed."

As she pulls me toward the house, she stops all of a sudden, motions to me to bend down, and whispers, "*I* think he's come back to live with us."

"Don't count on it," I whisper back, but I can't help wondering if that's what's going on. Has he already said something to my mom? Is that why she's acting so happy all of a sudden? It doesn't make sense, but I don't know how else to explain it. Anyways, I can't say it's what I want. But I can't say it isn't.

When we enter the living room, it's like Time Warp meets "Do I know you." I mean, there's my dad sitting in "his" chair, the one he sat in every night for the first ten years of my life, but which has been my mom's chair ever since he left. At first glance, he looks like he belongs there, like his leaving is just something I dreamed. That's the Time Warp part. But then, come on, who *is* this dude in the tie and button-down shirt? I mean, even if he wears ties now, why is he wearing one in our house? What happened to his leather jacket? Who *is* he?

My mom (her hair is up) sits all the way at one end of the couch, as if there are six other people squeezed in next to her and she's about to fall off the edge. She fidgets with the three magazines she left on the coffee table, while Megan sits way at the other end of the couch, studying my cell phone like there's going to be a quiz on it tomorrow.

"Hey," I say to her, "that's *my* phone."

"What do *you* need it for? It's not like you have a life."

"Meggie, talk nice to your brother," my dad says,

which makes me snort and Megan roll her eyes so big you could probably see them in Michigan.

And we don't live anywhere near Michigan.

I go to grab it out of Megan's hands and, miraculously, it buzzes.

It's a text from Joe. **Come over right now,** it reads.

Give me 15 mins, I text back.

That's how long I think I can stand being in this house with my dad not talking about why he's come back, one sister hoping he'll stay forever and the other sister wishing he'd drop dead, and my mom having morphed into some kind of TV mom from Nick at Nite.

As for me, I know I said part of me wanted him back, but I don't know where that part is right now. I feel as confused about his being here as I do thinking about girls and dogs.

I half listen to my dad tell my mom about his job in Rochester, which is where he's lived for the past year and a half and is about as far as he could get away from us and still be in the same state, and how he's cleaned up his act, and yeah, he still has his Harley, but he doesn't get out on it as much as he used to, because, you know, his job . . . and stuff . . . keeps him busy.

That's the way he says it: "'Cause, you know, my job" (PAUSE) "and stuff" (PAUSE) "keeps me busy."

My mom does not ask what the "stuff" is, and I don't either, because

1. I'm only half listening.
2. I want to get over to Joe's house.
3. I don't care.

Then again, maybe neither of us asks because

4. We don't want to know the answer.

All this talk about his job in Rochester makes me start to think maybe he wants us to move there with him. I don't know which would be worse, his moving back in with us or us moving there. Okay, it's a no-brainer. There's no way I'm packing up and leaving Paintbrush Falls and my friends to move to the Middle of Nowhere, New York, and hang out with my dad and his buddies from Xerox.

And by the way, with all his yak-yak-yak about his job, he hasn't even said what it is he *does*.

"I've got ice cream from Stewart's," my mom announces in this chirpy Nick at Nite voice. "Bear Paw. Your favorite."

My dad nods his head. "Yeah, I like Bear Paw all right. You remembered."

"Well, sure," my mom says. "I may hate your guts, but I still remember what you like."

My dad laughs at this, and so does my mom, and I think, *People, can this get any weirder?*

As tempting as the Bear Paw ice cream is (it also happens to be my favorite, but I'm not telling my dad that), I've got to get out of here.

"That was Joe texting just now," I say. "I have to go over to his house. We're, uh, working on a paper."

"A paper?" my mom asks. Busted! I completely forgot it was summer.

"Not a paper *exactly*," I say, thinking fast. "Well, you know how we, uh, you know how we write that humor column for the school newspaper?" (This part is true.) "Well, we have this summer project of writing a funny story that, like, you know, continues. . . ."

"You mean it's serialized?" (*Yes!* Work with me, Mom.)

"Right. And we should have been working on it before this, but we didn't, and we really need to get started, because we have to have six parts written before school starts, and Mr. Daly wants to see the first three parts before the end of July." (Lies, lies, and more lies.) "And Joe's going away on vacation tomorrow." (True.)

My mom is hesitating, but my dad jumps in and says, "It's okay. I'll be here for a week."

"Just a *week*?" Jessie whines. "Are you going to stay here with us?"

"I'll be out at my buddy Del's."

"Aww," says Jessie.

"We'll grab us some quality time later on,

Skeeze, just you and me. You go ahead over to Joe's."

Oh boy, just what I want. Grabbing some quality time with my dad.

"Thanks," I go, and I'm out of there before the scoop has hit the Bear Paw.

Here's something I've noticed. I'm thinking this on the way over to Joe's. Ever since my dad left, I only call him "my dad." Even in my head. I don't call him "Dad" anymore. I don't know what that means. I still call Penny "Penny," and not "my dog." And even Grandpa, who died a few years ago, I don't say, "my grandpa." But my dad, it's like he doesn't have a name anymore.

At least, not a name I want to call him.

The Half-True Story of
Penny the Dog

By the time I get to Joe's house, a party's going on. The gang is down in the basement with *good* music and Cheetos and four half-gallons of ice cream (including Bear Paw, so I'm not even missing out). And it's not just the gang who's there, but Kelsey and Zachary and Becca, who is wearing shorts so short I have to look away.

"My invitation must have gotten lost in the mail," I say to Joe as I grab a handful of Cheetos.

"Now, Skeezie," Joe says, wagging a finger at me, "don't be all sulky. It's not manly. *Nobody* got an invitation. This is what we call spontaneous."

Becca pats a spot on the couch next to her and says, "Sit."

Like a dog, I obey.

"Guess what," she says, turning and brushing Cheetos dust off the front of my shirt. What is it with girls and food placement? I was perfectly happy to have Cheetos dust on my shirt.

"What?" I ask obediently. I'll probably start wagging my tail next.

"We're going," she says.

"You're moving?" I ask. "You just moved back here, like, six months ago."

It's true. Becca had lived in Paintbrush Falls, down the street from Addie, when she was little. Then she moved away and showed up again, six months ago, in the middle of seventh grade. I would never have figured she would be friends of any of us. She was all attitude and OMG and the right shoes. And she was always busting Addie's chops. But then it turned out that she actually looked up to Addie and even missed her, because they had played together a lot as kids. And ever since the end of school, she's been hanging out with us, and now I am sitting next to her on the couch in Joe's basement, trying not to look at her legs.

You know that LIFE IS GOOD T-shirt? I need one that says LIFE IS WEIRD.

Becca laughs. "It was *seven* months ago," she says. "And we're not moving away. We're going to the shelter to get a dog. Clay caved."

"I don't understand that last sentence," I tell her. "Clay cave?"

"You're so *funny*," Becca says, laughing again. "Clay is my stepfather, and he's the one who's been saying we shouldn't have a dog because they're too much work. But my mom and I convinced him, and so we're going next week when he gets back from a business trip, and we're getting a dog!"

At this point, she squeals and does this girly thing with her shoulders and head that's like a mini cheerleader move, and I go, "Yay, dog!" before I know what I'm doing. And this gets her laughing really hard, and she puts her hand on my knee and says, "Seriously, you are *so* funny."

All of a sudden, I get hit with a spray of seltzer and Zachary's all like, "Oh, I'm so sorry, Skeezie." And Joe is laughing like a maniac, because he's the one who convinced Zachary to shake the can before he opened it, and I think, *And I'm supposed to be the immature one around here?*

I jump up and wipe myself off with one of the throw pillows on the couch, which Joe is grabbing at and shouting, "Not the *Phantom of the Opera* pillow!" And now Becca is laughing like an even bigger maniac than Joe, and everybody seems to think the whole thing couldn't be funnier if it was on Comedy Central. Everybody but Zachary, that is, who is so nice and sincere that he's still apologizing a half hour later.

Anyways, the point is that my conversation with Becca about her getting a dog gets derailed, along with her hand on my knee; and, once everybody calms down after what will live on as the Notorious Seltzer Incident, all anybody wants to talk about are their Big Family Vacations. Addie's not going away on hers until August, but she is leaving tomorrow to visit her grandma for a week. As it turns out, Bobby and his dad are heading off for their camping trip tomorrow, too. And Joe and his family are leaving for Montreal. Or as Joe insists on putting it, *"Nous allons à la métropole."*

Much of the time, I have no idea what Joe's talking about—even when he's speaking English.

I sit there feeling miserable. Not only do I *not* want to hear about everybody's jolly times with their happy families, I don't want to think about the fact that my three best friends are all going to be away at the same time. For an entire week, they are leaving me here jerking sodas in Paintbrush Falls while they go out to see the world and have fun. Talk about rotten stinkin' planning on their parts. The least they could have done was consult with me first!

And to make matters worse, knowing that Becca is getting an actual dog makes me realize how much I want a dog and how much I miss Penny, and how both those things have been true for six years—almost half my entire life.

Somehow, even though everybody's been moving around, about a half hour later Becca and I end up sitting on the couch next to each other again. And somehow she's picked up on the fact of me being miserable, possibly because instead of saying anything, I have just set a new world record for the Number of Cheetos Eaten By a Thirteen-Year-Old in Thirty Minutes or Less.

She bumps her shoulder against mine. "I'm not going away on vacation, either," she says.

"Yeah, but you're getting a dog."

"Yay, dog," she goes, smiling at me like we've just shared our first secret.

Is Steffi right? Does Becca actually *like* me? Is this possible?

"You should get a dog, too," she says.

I don't go into the million and one reasons this is not going to happen. Instead, I tell her, "I had a dog once. When I was seven."

"What happened to him?" she asks.

"Her. Her name was Penny. She ran away and I never saw her again."

Becca looks like she's going to cry. I don't know if it's because of Penny in particular, or she's just one of those people who gets all weepy when anything bad happens to a dog.

"Did she—was she—you know, like, okay?"

james howe

I shrug. "I don't know. Like I said, I never saw her again. So how should I know if she was okay or not? She never turned up dead or anything, that I heard about anyways, but . . ."

Becca puts her hand on my arm. "I'm sorry, Skeezie," she says. "Really."

I like the feel of her hand on my arm and I like the sound of her voice when she says she's sorry, but I'm not sure I want to say anything else. If I tell her the whole story, I'll end up bawling, because— you probably guessed this already—I'm one of those people who gets all weepy when anything bad happens to a dog. Especially when the dog was mine.

Plus, she's a girl. And like I said, I don't know how to talk around girls.

But somehow Becca gets me talking. I don't tell her the whole story, just the part I can tell and not get all choked up about.

Penny was a mutt, I tell her, a stray somebody found out along Route 9 and brought to the shelter. When my dad and I went there to pick out a dog, I took one look at her and said, "That one!"

"Let's look at them all first, Skeezo," my dad said, but I wouldn't budge. I knelt down in front of Penny's cage and put my face right up to the chain link where you're not supposed to, and she stuck out her big old taffy tongue and started licking my nose like it was some kind of doggie lollipop. It tickled. I giggled. And my dad said, "Done deal."

Penny had some other name the shelter gave her, something dumb like Princess or Pickles or something, but I said we had to name her Penny because she had penny-colored hair, just like Joe's mom. And *her* name is Penny, and I always thought that was so cool. I guess my Penny must have had some golden retriever in her, but when you're seven years old and you finally get the dog you've been blowing out birthday candles for your whole life, you don't care what kind she is. All that matters is that she's yours. And that she has a good name. Penny was a good name.

My dad had already built the doghouse and put up the kennel, so Penny moved right in when we got back home. I wanted her in the house with me, curled up at my feet under the kitchen table while I did my homework and snoring her head off next to me in my bed at night. But I'd already lost that fight. My mom said no way. She didn't want a dog in the first place, because she figured she'd be the one to take care of it. And she for sure didn't want one in the house.

"I've got two kids already—three, counting your dad—and another one on the way," she'd tell me, "and we are *not* getting a dog. Period. End of discussion."

Of course, it wasn't the end of the discussion. I kept on bringing it up every chance I got, and my dad was quick to take my side. He'd had a dog when he was growing up, and he believed that every boy should have a dog. I don't know where that left girls, but that wasn't my concern at the time.

The truth is, getting a dog was one of the things my parents fought about. They fought about a lot of things, but the fact that getting a dog was one of them made me feel guilty, like their fighting was my fault. So when my dad ended one fight with, "We're getting the boy a dog, Allie, and that's the end of it!" I didn't know whether to cheer or hang my head.

He let me help him build the doghouse, and he took me with him to the Home Depot to pick up the chain-link fence to make the kennel. Two days later we were at the shelter and my dad was signing the papers that made Penny my dog.

"I had her for three months, one week, and four days. She got out of her kennel and ran away and I never saw her again," I tell Becca as if this is the end of the story, even though it's only half the truth.

Becca's eyes are wet. "How did she get out?" she asks.

I hesitate before answering. "Dug her way under the fence," I say, crossing over from half a truth to a full-out lie.

Becca shakes her head and wipes the tears away with the back of her hand.

"You should totally come with us," she says.

"Huh?"

"When we go to the shelter next week. You should totally come with us."

"Nah," I say. "I don't think so."

Suddenly, Becca's eyes light up and she's like, "You really *have* to, Skeezie. Oh, please. You know you want to. *Please.*" Now she does that pouty-girl thing I hate, but somehow it looks good on Becca, especially when it's directed at me and she's asking me to go with her to pick out a dog.

"I might have to work . . . or take care of Megan and Jessie or . . ."

"Or clean out your sock drawer. Oh, come on, it will be so fun! We'll go when you're *not* working or taking care of your sisters or—"

"Or cleaning out my sock drawer," I say, and we both laugh.

"So you'll come?"

I nod and go, "Yeah. I'll come."

"Yay!" she says, clapping her hands. And then she reaches one of those hands out to me and the next thing I know I'm dancing with Becca

Wrightsman. It's the first time I've danced with a girl. Ever.

I try to ignore my friends hooting and making a big deal out of the fact that I, Skeezie Tookis, am dancing at all and think, *Maybe it'll be okay being on my own for a week. If being on my own means being with Becca.*

All Shook Up

Saturday my mom and I have to work, so my dad is spending the day with the girls. He's taking them out to Water Slide World. I actually like Water Slide World and would normally feel bad about not getting to go, especially on a hot day like this, but right now I feel lucky that I have to work, because it means being spared so-called quality time with my dad. Let the girls have it, is what I say. Jessie will take all she can get, and Megan will have a good time sulking.

I start the day mowing Addie's lawn, which totally sucks because I have to watch her load her stuff into her mom's Volvo, then wave at her while they drive off to the Trailways station and yell, "Have fun!" like I mean it. When what I really want to yell is, "Have fun while I stay here and get all stinky and sweaty cutting your grass in the hundred-degree heat!"

"Oh, I will!" she calls back, waving like the queen of England or something.

"I'll bring you out some lemonade when I get back from dropping Addie off!" Addie's mom shouts before rolling up her window and disappearing into her nice *air-conditioned* car.

Addie's dad is inside the house practicing his cello, which I can't hear because of the noise from the mower, but I know because he told me, "If you need me, I'll be inside practicing my cello," like it's a normal father thing to be doing on a Saturday. My dad—and probably 99 percent of the dads in America—would be inside drinking beers and watching football. Not that I think that's a great thing. Personally, I hate football and the smell of beer, so I could easily end up in the other one percent, although it's more likely I'd be practicing my electric guitar (if I had one) and not the cello.

Thinking this gets me to singing "'You ain't nothin' but a hound dog'" nice and loud because the lawn mower drowns out everything, and this gets me to thinking about going with Becca to the shelter next week to look at dogs. I'm going to admit something right now, and you've got to promise not to tell anybody, especially my friends, but since they're all out of town, I figure it's safe to say: I could hardly get to sleep last night thinking about going with Becca next week. At first, I figured it was about looking at dogs, but every time I tried picturing a dog's face, it was Becca's face that showed up instead.

And then I got to remembering what Becca was like before she and Addie started being friends again, how she could act snobby and mean a lot of the time, and it felt weird having girlfriend-type thoughts about her. It feels weird having girlfriend-type thoughts, period, but about Becca? Super weird.

But just wait. Later that afternoon at the Candy Kitchen things get *double* super weird. With a cherry on top.

It starts with this text I get from Becca. I'm not supposed to be texting while I'm at work, but I keep my phone under the counter and just check it every once in a while, so it's not like I'm always on it. Still, I try to keep it hidden from Steffi, because I don't want her turning into a boss-type person and reminding me of the rules of employment and stuff like that. Not that I think she'd do that, but you never know.

Anyways, the joint is jumping, probably because it's so hot out and everybody wants cold drinks and ice cream, and we've only got me and Steffi and this dude named Henry working out front, with Donny back in the kitchen. Henry's a high school senior and he's a nice enough guy, but he's kind of a space cadet. Like, he'll write down every little detail of your order, repeat it to you twice, and then mess it up. Guaranteed. So Steffi's got me working the fountain. Sodas. Ice cream sundaes. Everything. It's a lot of pressure because, like I said, the joint is jumping, but it also feels way cool because it's the most responsibility I've ever been given and Steffi is trusting me not to mess up, Henry-style.

So anyways. The text. It reads: **Tues noon animal shelter ok?**

I think fast. I don't work on Tuesdays, so as long as I don't have to take care of Megan and Jessie, I'm cool.

ok, I text back, to which I get a fast **YAY!** in return.

YAY! All caps. Exclamation point.

So now I'm trying to make five kinds of sundaes and all I can think about is going to the shelter to look at *dogs* with this *girl* who might actually like me, and it's all I can do to keep the hot fudge from running all over the floor and making a gigantic Henry-size mess.

To make matters worse, Becca shows up about twenty minutes later with two of her non-Addie friends, Royal Wilkins and Sara Jakes. Royal and Sara were bffs with Becca until she started hanging out with Addie and then they dropped the *b* and one of the *f*s.

Okay, now we're starting to move into DSWWACOT (double-super-weird-with-a-cherry-on-top) territory.

So they walk in, all linky-arms and girly, with

Becca on the end farthest away from me. I notice there's something different about Becca right away. It's not just all the makeup she's wearing, which is back to what it was pre-Addie. It's the way she's moving across the room and giggling and saying *omigod* every other word. Mostly it's how she is *ignoring me.* If I didn't know better, I'd say we were right back in the hall at Paintbrush Falls Middle School between classes.

"Hey," I say into the air.

Becca's half smile lets me know that she's in the same air as the *hey,* but the nonsmiling half makes me think she doesn't want anyone else to know it.

What's up with that?

Seriously.

The three of them move right past me and take the booth in the back—*our* booth, the one normally occupied by me (when I'm not working) and the gang (who, let me remind you, are all out of town as of a few hours ago)—as if, *as if,* they own it. I mean, fine, Becca has spent some time in that booth, but Royal and Sara? They do *not* belong there, dude.

Okay, so I'm trying to live and let live and all that good stuff, but the whole deal is rubbing me the wrong way. Then my phone buzzes.

hi

It's from Becca.

I glance over and she's not even looking in my direction.

Are you with me here? There is some serious weirdness happening. But wait. The Cherry on Top arrives in about five minutes.

So do I text back or not?

I see Steffi eyeing me with my phone in my hand. I decide on *not* and quickly put it back under the counter.

Next thing I know, I'm in the middle of making a black-and-white shake when I see Steffi walking over from Becca's table.

"One dish mint chocolate chip, one vanilla egg cream, and one Dr Pepper float," she says, sliding the order across the counter at me.

"A Dr P float?" I go. "Really?"

Steffi winks at me. "I told you she likes you," she says.

I shrug and look over at Becca, who's still not making eye contact. At least, not with me. She's got her eyes on Royal, across the table from her, and even from here I can see that she's saying, "Omigod!" Pretty soon they're all checking out each other's nail polish and probably all going *omigod.* Whatever. I'm still hoping Becca will look my way and say hi with her face and not just her phone.

I see her looking down under the table, and the next thing I know my phone buzzes.

It's Becca. Naturally. Or should I say: weirdly.

love this song

I listen to hear what's playing. Steffi must have just put on this playlist we put together for her iPod—half stuff she likes, half stuff I like. Right now, the King is crooning about being all shook up, a little mixed up, and feelin' fine. Except for the feelin' fine part, he could be singing about me.

I take a chance.
one of my faves, I text her back.
I figured
u like elvis?
sometimes
but u love this song
totally
A hand taps my shoulder.
Steffi.

"Come on, Big E," she says to me, giving me this look that says, *Give me a break.* "Don't turn me into the evil authority figure. Look around; I'm dying here. I can't keep up. Henry just screwed up two burger orders and Donnie's cursing *me* out in the kitchen like it's my fault. And I've got to pee. Bad. So here."

She slides a tray at me, which means, *You take the food to the table.*

Only in this case it's not a table, it's a booth. I'm just finishing up the Dr Pepper float. Lucky me: I get to deliver the drinks and ice cream to Becca, Royal, and Sara.

As I start loading everything onto the tray, the door flies open, this time knocking over the umbrella stand, and who walks in but the Cherry on Top: the one and only Kevin Hennessey.

"Well, if it isn't my favorite soda *jerk!*" he goes, flashing a big smile at his own cleverness as if he had just come up with this line instead of repeating it for, like, the hundredth time this summer.

I do my best to ignore him, which isn't always the best strategy with Kevin, because it usually just encourages him to ramp it up. Which is what happens now.

"Looks like you're busy," he says in this mock-friendly way. "Maybe I can help you out. Huh, Squeeze, can I help you out, huh?"

I'm coming around the end of the soda fountain holding a tray up in one hand, the way I've been taught to do, trying to balance a dish of mint chocolate chip ice cream, a vanilla egg cream, and a Dr Pepper float when Kevin lunges.

"Careful!" he goes, looking like he's going to

grab the tray but stopping just short of making contact.

I jump back and the tray goes flying. Nobody gets hurt, but there's ice cream and seltzer, Dr P, and broken glass everywhere.

Some people gasp.

Some people laugh.

One of *those* people is Becca Wrightsman. The sound of her laughter cuts right through Elvis's singing. All shook up. Oh yeah.

Total Mess-up Loser

After the laughing dies down, I sweep up the broken glass, mop up the mess, go back behind the counter, and remake the order for Becca, Royal, and Sara. I wait for Steffi to get out of the john so she can take it to their booth. I don't say thanks when she does.

I don't respond when Kevin says, "It wasn't *my* fault, I was just tryin' to help."

I don't look over when Becca calls out, "Awesome float!"

I don't speak or text or pick up my phone for the rest of the afternoon.

I get by on grunts and shrugs.

The Candy Kitchen doesn't stay open at night anymore. Not even on a Saturday. If anybody wants ice cream, they go out to the mall or to Stewart's. By five o'clock, the town is pretty much dead. So from five to six, which is when we close, it's often just Steffi, Donny, and me cleaning up, with an occasional straggler coming in for a hand-packed pint or a box of chocolates.

The other times I've worked up to closing I've liked it. Donny's back in the kitchen while Steffi and I wipe down the tables, fill up the napkin holders, and mop the floor. We shoot the breeze and make up stories about the stragglers, like this guy is buying chocolates for his wife because he spent the afternoon with his girlfriend and he feels guilty, or that guy is bringing ice cream home to his kid who's sick in bed. For some reason, it's usually guys who come in between five and six. When we know one of the stragglers, it's not as much fun. It's best when it's a stranger and you can make up anything you want.

But tonight nothing about it is fun. When somebody comes in and buys something, Steffi waits on them and we don't talk about them after they leave. Our playlist is still playing, but we don't talk about the songs like we usually do, and I don't sing along to Elvis, even when it's a song I know by heart.

I just want to go home. But then I think about it and I don't want to go home, because I'm worried my dad will be there and I don't want to see him. I don't even want to see my mom or my sisters. If I want to see anybody, it's my friends, and they're not here. I can't even call or text Bobby (who's the best one to talk to because he actually listens and doesn't jump right in and tell you what to do), because he's at this stupid camp in the Adirondacks where there's no cell phone service or Internet. What kind of freakin' vacation is *that*?

I don't know what's worse, the way Becca acted like she didn't know me (except as a soda *jerk* who makes an *awesome* float), or how Kevin embarrassed me in front of everybody and made me mess up so bad even Henry called me out on it. Steffi tried telling me it was okay, that it happens to everybody, but I just grunted and shrugged. I'm not everybody. I'm me, total mess-up loser Schuyler Tookis—yeah, Schuyler's my real name;

you didn't seriously think my parents named me Skeezie, did you?—who can't even get a girl to like him or keep a bully like Kevin Hennessey from busting his chops.

Sometimes I get so mad I just want to punch Kevin's lights out. Or I picture myself picking up one of the heavy napkin holders sitting on the counter and smashing it down on my phone like it's Becca's heart until it's broken into a thousand pieces. But I don't, because I'm pretty sure that's what my dad would do.

It's quarter to six and Steffi says, "Why don't you get out of here, Elvis?"

I shrug.

"Tomorrow will be a better day," she says.

I shake my head.

"You *are* working tomorrow, right?"

For the first time in hours, I speak. "If I don't quit first."

"Come on, Big E," she says. "You can't quit and leave me here with Henry. Get a good night's sleep and I'll see you at twelve. Okay?"

"Whatever," I mumble.

I grab my phone from under the counter, shove it in my pocket, nod in Steffi's direction, and shuffle out the door.

It looks like maybe it's going to rain. I pull the phone out of my pocket, thinking I'll text Joe, see what's up, tell him about what happened. I see that there are a whole bunch of texts from Becca. Most of them say the same thing.

sorry

I delete them all.

I don't even remember what I was going to say to Joe. I look up and down Main Street. I think about all the different ways I can walk home and ask myself which way will take me the longest.

Baby

It starts raining hard the minute I step out from under the Candy Kitchen awning, and even though I'm feeling crummy, it isn't the kind of crummy where you want to walk around in the rain feeling sorry for yourself. It's more the kind where you want to get home in a hurry so you can yell at your sisters to make their *own* stinkin' supper and then grab a big bag of Doritos and hole up in your room and tell everybody to go away and leave you alone. Unless of course your stinkin' excuse for a father happens to be there, in which case you might reconsider walking around in the rain feeling sorry for yourself.

Turns out he isn't here.

Neither is my mom.

Jessie, wearing a Water Slide World T-shirt and matching visor, greets me with a big hug around the legs and shouts at me like I'm in the next county, "We had the *best* day ever!"

"*Except* for the fact that we couldn't go on *any* of the really *exciting* stuff because *Jessie* is too *little!*" Megan chimes in from the couch, where she's sprawled out watching some dumb show on TV. I notice she's wearing this sparkly LOVE PINK T-shirt that she's been begging our mom to get her for freakin' ever. It's entirely possible that *love pink* were her first words.

"Where'd you get that shirt?" I ask as if I don't know the answer.

When she doesn't say anything, I kick at her butt and she squeals, "Stop it, Skeezie!" before going, "Where do you think? Daddy."

"Wow," I say. "Wonder when I get *my* new shirt."

Megan grunts. I kick her butt. She kicks the air. I walk into the kitchen, where nothing—like food preparation, for instance—is happening.

"Where's Mom?" I ask Jessie, who follows me in. "She's not supposed to leave you guys alone."

Jessie points to the fridge, and I spot a note stuck behind a Water Slide World magnet.

"Your dad and I are going out to supper so we can talk," it reads. "I brought home pizza for you to heat up and there's salad stuff. I told the girls they can stay up until 9:30. NO LATER! Thanks, baby. I owe you one."

Other than the fact that my mother called me "baby"—seriously, how creepy is that?—I'm cool with her note, I guess, although it bothers me that she left the girls on their own when I'd get into serious trouble for doing the same thing. I mean, no way would she have done this before my dad showed up. He is *so* messing with her head.

Anyways, pizza's easy. Jessie likes to help make salad. And by the time my mom gets back from "talking," I'll be in my room with a big bag of corn chips and a sign on the door that says DO NOT DISTURB.

It almost works out. Too bad that:

1. Jessie gets sick after supper, and I spend the next two hours holding her head over the toilet and then reading

to her until she falls asleep a little after nine.

2. Megan uses the computer without permission and tells me there's a picture of me on Facebook mopping up ice cream with the caption, "Soda Jerk Squeezie T. would make a good jantor." Kevin may have entered the world of cyberbullying, but he still hasn't mastered spelling.

3. Becca texts to say that she saw the picture and doesn't think it's funny.

4. I delete her text, and

5. We're out of chips.

Oh, on top of which:

6. My mom gets home at 9:32, yells at Megan for not being in bed yet, yells at me for playing my music too loud, yells at all of us for leaving the kitchen a mess (which, other than a pizza box lying

open on a counter, it isn't), slams the
door to her bedroom, and yells a bunch
of words I'm not going to put down here
but you can use your imagination.

I was hoping I could convince her to run me out
to the Stewart's and spring for a big bag of Doritos
using her employee discount, but when I hear her
stop cursing and start crying, I figure I can just forget about the "one" she owes me.

I'm mentally ripping up her note when I hear
Jessie knocking at my door informing me she's
going to be sick again.

About an hour later my head hits my pillow and
I fall asleep to the rattling of the air conditioner my
mom got at a tag sale for ten bucks, telling myself
that I'm not a bad person just because I hope my
friends are all having totally sucky vacations.

How My Mother Feels About Garlic Knots

The next morning Jessie is fine. She throws up sometimes, that's all. But after she and Megan go over to Megan's friend Kyra's house, my mom is all on my case about how I didn't tell her that Jessie was sick the minute she slammed home from the Olive Garden last night. Here I am thinking I deserve a medal for holding my little sister's head for two hours while she pukes, but instead I get grief because I failed to interrupt my mom midmeltdown with a newsflash.

And what's even worse, according to her, is that I didn't call her at the restaurant so she could race right home.

I say, "Mom."

She says, "What is wrong with you, Skeezie?"

I say, "What's wrong with *me*?"

She says, "Your sister might have been really ill."

I say, "Yeah, but she wasn't."

She says, "But you didn't know that."

I say, "But I did. Jessie throws up. Remember?"

She says, "But I'm her mother."

I say, "Yeah, and I'm her brother. And I took care of it. Even *after* you got home. And she's fine."

She doesn't say anything to that. She just sits at the kitchen table, downing her third cup of coffee, and then calls my dad a bad name. At least I assume she's talking about my dad.

I glance at the clock over the stove.

"I gotta go to work," I tell her, thinking no matter what Kevin Hennessey or Becca Wrightsman or anybody else has in store for me today, it's got to be better than this.

"You want to know why he's here?" she says.

"Not really," I say.

"Oh, it's good," she says. "It's rich."

"That's nice," I say.

"You think he wants to come back to us?" she says. "Is that what you think?"

She pulls a cigarette out of her purse.

"Could you not smoke in the house?" I say.

"Who made you the mayor?" she says.

She puts the cigarette back.

"He came back," she says, "to get a divorce."

I shrug.

"He came back to get a divorce because he wants to get married to some girl he met in Rochester."

"Okay."

"He owes me money and he hardly ever sees you kids and he comes back wearing a *tie* and tells me he wants a divorce so he can marry some girl in Rochester."

My cereal has turned to mush, which I hate. I pick up the bowl and dump the whole thing in the garbage. It's disgusting, but less disgusting than eating it.

"So I guess I don't have to spend any quality time with him," I say, keeping my back to her so she doesn't see the part of me that was kind of hoping he was coming back for good. Which, to be honest, totally confuses me.

"He's still your father," she says. "He has a legal

right to see you. And besides, he wants to talk with you about something. He wouldn't say what, just said it was time you two talked man to man."

Omigod, not The Talk. Anything but The Talk.

"Well, I can't see him today," I say. "I'm working the lunch shift, and then Zachary asked me to come over and hang out. And then—"

"He's going fishing with Del today," she says. Del is an old high school friend of my dad's. "He wants to spend the day with you tomorrow. I told him fine."

My cheeks burn so hot you could fry eggs on them. "Who told you that you could tell him fine?" I say, turning to face her. "Maybe I don't want to see my dad. Or maybe, just maybe, *I* want to decide when I'm going to see him."

"Don't get all het up," my mom says, using one of my grandma's expressions. "You can spare one day out of your busy social life to see your father."

This is too stinkin' much!

"Social life?" I go. "I'm working all the time, remember? And when I'm not working, I'm taking care of *your* daughters. You're out eating garlic knots while I'm watching Jessie upchuck pizza into the toilet. It's a good thing it flushes, thanks to money *I* earned!"

My mom looks at me like I slapped her. "Do you have any idea how hard it is being an adult?" she screams. "I can't handle it! I'm thirty-two years old and I feel like I'm fifty! I can't help it that I need your help, Skeezie! I can't help it that your father left me here with you three kids and hardly comes around and when he does it's so he can get married to someone else. Some girl in Rochester! Some girl he knows in this life he has in Rochester that doesn't include us!

"And for your information, I *hate* garlic knots! They are doughy and greasy and I was *not* eating them last night! I was *not* having a good time! I was sitting across the table from your father in his ridiculous tie wondering why I was hoping he wanted to come back to me when I hate him even more than I hate garlic knots! Do you get this? Do you get any of this?"

It is not fun watching your mother have a nervous breakdown, even if you have seen it before. You never know what to say.

"Yeah, okay," I tell her. "You hate garlic knots, I get it."

Clearly, this is not the right thing to say. She bursts into tears and runs out of the kitchen.

And now it is time for me to go to work at the Candy Kitchen. I swear, if Kevin Hennessey shows up today, I am going to have to do him bodily harm. I am not normally the violent type, but sometimes a person can only take so much.

Life is funny, and I don't mean ha-ha. What I mean, Little E, is that even though it may not seem like it at the time, sometimes things happen for a reason. Like that summer. If my friends hadn't all been away the week my dad was in town, I probably wouldn't have gotten to talking about things with Steffi the way I did.

I was only thirteen, so I wasn't used to talking about serious stuff all that much, but the closest I'd ever had to what you might call heavy conversations were with Bobby and Joe and Addie. They had become my best friends after Addie sent me a secret Valentine in second grade. Up until then I didn't really have any friends at all, except for Penny and she was a dog. I don't like admitting this to you, because I don't want you getting the idea that you should follow in my footsteps, but I was kind of a troublemaker before that secret Valentine. I did things to get noticed, things that weren't very nice. So big surprise that I didn't have any friends, right? But Addie, well, she was this no-nonsense person—she still is; you'll get to know her because she's still one of my best friends—and she just said, in so many words, "Skeezie, I think you're nice even if you are kind of a jerk."

The other thing about Addie is that she's strong. When she makes up her mind about something, that's it! I don't know why, but she made up her mind that I was going to be her friend and she wasn't about to have a friend who was a jerk, so what could I do? I became her friend and stopped being a jerk. And because Bobby and Joe were already her friends, I became their friend, too.

Anyway, like I said, I think there are reasons that things happen when they do. Like Penny running away a couple of months before Addie asked me to be her friend. I had finally known what it was like to have a friend, even if she had four legs and stinky breath, and I wasn't ready to be lonely again.

And then near the end of second grade, Bobby's mom got real sick. I didn't know just how sick at the time, and I couldn't make sense of it when she died the summer between second and third grade. But when we went back to school that fall, I knew that being friends was the best thing Addie and Joe and I could do for Bobby. And so we became the Gang of Five, even though there were only four of us. I was the one who came up with that name, because I thought it was funny, and it stuck. And *we* stuck. Up until then, it was as if we'd been held together by Scotch tape, but once we were the Gang of Five, we were stuck to each other with Krazy Glue.

After my dad left when I was ten, it was Addie and Joe and Bobby who kept me from running away. Whether I wanted to run off to find my dad or to make him worry so much he'd come back home, who knows. But it was the gang that convinced me to stay.

They were always there for me—until the week I needed them most.

The Skeezie-Steffi Dialogues: Rain

Steffi: Rain makes me sad.

Skeezie: Always?

Steffi: No, not always. Sometimes. This is one
            of those times.

Skeezie: Yeah, we had enough rain last night.
            Why's it got to rain today?

Steffi: It's not the *fact* of the rain that makes
            me sad.

Skeezie: Is it because it's keeping the customers
            away and there go our tips?

Steffi: No. I'm sorry we won't be getting any
            tips, but I don't mind having a slow day.
            It's a mood thing. I get melancholy. Does
            that ever happen to you? You're a guy
            and you're only thirteen, so probably not.

Skeezie: Who says? I get moods. Remember me
            telling you about sitting out in Penny's
            doghouse? I do that when I'm down.

Steffi:	Mm.
Skeezie:	(singing) "I get so lonely, I get so lonely I could die."
Steffi:	(laughing) That's an Elvis song, right?
Skeezie:	"Heartbreak Hotel."
Steffi:	Is that how you feel sometimes? So lonely you could die?
Skeezie:	Nah. I just like the song.
Steffi:	I feel that way sometimes.
Skeezie:	I thought you had a boyfriend.
Steffi:	I do. But that doesn't mean I don't get lonely. We can even be together and I get lonely. Crazy, right?
Skeezie:	I dunno. What do I know? I'm a guy and I'm only thirteen.
Steffi:	Alex wants us to get married.
Skeezie:	Dude. Don't do it. You're nineteen.
Steffi:	I know, right?
Skeezie:	My parents were nineteen when they got married.
Steffi:	Really?
Skeezie:	Uh-huh.

Steffi: Wow.

Skeezie: Yeah, wow. Don't be crazy like that.

Steffi: But if they hadn't gotten married, they wouldn't have had you.

Skeezie: You got a point there.

Steffi: You and your sisters.

Skeezie: Yeah, me and my sisters, and a big, fat broken home.

Steffi: Hey, my home's broken, too. And my parents were a lot older than yours when they got married. Maybe age has nothing to do with it.

Skeezie: Maybe. I don't know. I think it does.

Steffi: I told Alex, what's your hurry, and he's, like, it's our only way out of here, Steff. And I'm, like, are you kidding me? There are plenty of ways out of here without getting married.

Skeezie: Why do you want out of here? It's not bad. Joe's always talking about breaking out of here, too, like Paintbrush Falls is prison or something.

Steffi: Alex doesn't know what he wants.

Skeezie: So what do you want?

Steffi: I don't want to get married, that's for
            sure. Not at nineteen. And I'm like you.
            I like Paintbrush Falls. I could see living
            here my whole life.

Skeezie: Me, too.

Steffi: Look, this place is dead. Why don't you
            take off? Aren't you seeing your dad later?

Skeezie: Tomorrow. He's out fishing with his friend
            Del. He doesn't care if it's raining or not,
            as long as the fish are biting. I hate fishing.

Steffi: (laughing) So do I.

Skeezie: It's so freakin' boring.

Steffi: I feel sorry for the fish.

Skeezie: I should get over to Zachary's. We're
            going to hang out.

Steffi: Have fun.

Skeezie: You still sad?

Steffi: A little. Alex and I are going to the
            movies tonight.

Skeezie: Maybe it'll cheer you up.

Steffi: Maybe it's why I'm sad.

Not a Victoria's Secret Tennis Ball

Zachary opens the door wearing one of his Joe lookalike outfits. Normally, this would make me laugh, but right now it just makes me miss Joe.

Greeting me with, "Oh, my goodness," Zachary tells me to get inside quickly and not drip on the rug because his mother's kind of fussy.

"Where's your umbrella?" he asks.

"I'm a kid," I tell him. "I don't own an umbrella."

Handing me a towel, which appears out of nowhere (seriously, they keep towels by the front door?), he says, "I own three. I love umbrellas. And we've been having so much rain lately!"

When I say nothing to this, he tells me, "I'm learning to make pizza."

"Cool," I go. "That must be why it smells so good in here."

Nodding, Zachary leads me to the kitchen, and five minutes later we're eating this amazing pizza with pineapples and chicken and ham on it.

"You made this?" I ask. "Yourself?"

"It's called Hawaiian pizza."

"Goes with the shirt," I say, nodding at what he's wearing.

Zachary giggles. He's such a geek, you've got to love him.

"Your mom is okay with you cooking when she's not here?"

"Oh, she's here," he says. "She's upstairs in her office. But she's cool with me cooking. I've been cooking my whole life."

"Me, too," I tell him. "Or it feels that way, anyway. Ever since my dad left—"

Just then, Zachary's phone buzzes and he squeals, "Ooh, it's Joe!" Reading it, he says, "Oh, my goodness, Joe is such a nut. You will never guess what he's doing!"

"Um, texting you while riding a roller coaster?"

Zachary's jaw drops. Literally. "How did you know that? That is so psychic!"

"Really? Is that really what he's doing?"

"Yes! He's on something called the Vampire and . . . oh, he's screaming now, look!"

Zachary thrusts his phone at me and I read, **EEEEEEEEEEEEEEEEEEEEEK!**

Pretty soon, Joe is off the ride, and he and Zachary are texting back and forth while I'm sitting there eating most of the rest of the pizza. I get to thinking how Joe texted me once this morning, which is how I knew he was going to an amusement park today, but he got off quickly. Maybe it was because he knows I have limited texts on my mom's cell phone plan, or maybe it's because he and Zachary have more to say to each other.

Whatever. By the time I leave a couple of hours later, the rain has stopped and I'm full of pizza, but for some reason I still feel hungry.

When I get home, I see my mom's car in the driveway. She must have gone in the back door, because otherwise she would have taken in the bag I spot by the front door. It's this Victoria's Secret shopping bag with *Skeezie* written on it in large purple marker. The first thing I wonder is how long has it been sitting there and who has seen it and concluded that I ordered a see-through nightie or something like that. Seriously, how weird does my life have to get before I have my own reality show?

I crumple the bag under my arm and hijack it to my bedroom before the girls can spot it and say anything. Trust me, Megan can sniff out a Victoria's Secret shopping bag like she's a bloodhound and it's raw hamburger.

In my room, I uncrumple the bag and pull out a tennis ball from layers of pink and purple tissue paper. A tennis ball. Not one with feathers or beads or frilly, girly stuff all over it. In other words, not a Victoria's Secret tennis ball. Just a plain old tennis ball. And it looks used.

Digging around for an explanation, I find one in the form of a card. There's an envelope that some-body's written *Bow wow!* on, and inside is a note:

Skeezie,
    This is for the dog you're

going to help me pick out on
Tuesday. I thought you might
like to play with her. Or him. My
mom and I will pick you up at
noon. She said we can go for
pizza after. Unless we have to go
right home because of the dog.
And then we can have pizza at
our house.

Look, I'm sorry about
laughing at you. It was stupid,
but I was with my friends and
you know how it goes sometimes.
Forgive?

XOXO,
Becca

First of all, I thought I was your friend, too. And
yeah, I guess I know how it goes, but it wasn't you
laughing at me that made me mad. It was you
ignoring me, and all that weird, secret texting,
like we're only friends (or whatever we are) when

you're not with your *other* friends who would go *Ew, how can you be friends with Skeezie?* if they ever found out.

I say all this in my head, knowing I'll never really say it to Becca. And then I reread her note and think how many times she's said she's sorry in her texts and how she still wants me to go pick out a dog with her. And have pizza together. And how she wrote:

XOXO

Part of me wants to take the note to show Steffi, because she'd probably be good at figuring this out, even if she doesn't know what to do about a boyfriend who wants her to be a teen bride, but it's still raining and it's really Bobby I want to ask, anyways. But he's time traveling in the Adirondacks back to the World Before Technology, where they're probably camping out in caves and eating bison meat or something.

So I grab my phone and text Joe.

What's up

About five minutes later, I get a response.

Comment ca va, frere de boucle d'oreille?

Seriously?

I text back: **???????**

French for How are you, earring brother. Duh.

Like I would know that.

U would if u were here.

I would not be texting u if I was there. Duh.

Per tetre.

???????

Means maybe. But I spelled it wrong. So what's happening?

I am going nuts.

This is not news.

LOL not. Do u think Becca likes me?

Who are u and what have u done with Skeezie?

She's hanging with Royal and Sara and ignoring me, then texts me, then invites me to go get a dog with her.

It's too soon for you two to start a family.

Her dog. Her get a dog.

Awww. Un chien pour Becca.

DO U THINK BECCA LIKES ME?

u don't have to shout. Yes, I do. Tho pls do not ask me why.

Really?

You are the expert on love, MEB. Ask yourself.

I did but I didn't know the answer. MEB?

Monsieur Earring Brother.

You're scary weird.

You're scarier weirder. And yes Becca likes u. It's obvious. Gotta go.

Another roller coaster?

That is so two hours ago. We are in the gift shop.

Buy me something Canadian.

I will bring u a moose.

I will name it Joe.

Merci. Ciao.

Ciao?

Universal language for see ya.

I put down the phone and look out the window. Joe and Steffi both say Becca likes me. And even if

she didn't talk to me at the Candy Kitchen yesterday, she texted me, right?

And she left me a tennis ball in a Victoria's
Secret bag and wrote

XOXO,
Becca

I pick up the ball and toss it from hand to hand,
thinking *xo, xo, xo, xo,* when Megan starts pounding at my door.

"Mom says supper's ready!" she shouts.

Amazing. Supper's ready, and for once this
summer, I'm not the one making it. Things are
looking up.

Betty & Pauls

When my dad shows up on Monday morning, he is not wearing a tie. He's got on his biking vest with LIVE TO RIDE written on the back and a shirt with torn-off sleeves. The tail of his tattoo dragon wraps up his arm. Even with the belly he's put on, he's still wiry and strong. He looks like the dad I remember.

He checks me out, too. "Nice," he says, eyeing my (formerly his) leather jacket, "but isn't it kind of hot for that?"

I ignore the question. Instead, I focus on the beat-up Ford Ranger sitting at the curb. "What's up with the truck?" I say. "What happened to the Beast?"

That was my dad's nickname for his Harley.

"Like I told you, I still got it. I just needed somethin' practical. Sucks on mileage, but I can get a lotta crap in the back of this baby. Come on, jump in."

I throw open the door and see that the Ranger

isn't in as bad shape inside as it looks on the out-side. There's junk on the floor—crushed cans, papers, crumpled-up bags—but otherwise it's respectable enough.

I fasten my seat belt and stare straight ahead.

"What do you feel like doing?" he asks as he turns the key in the ignition.

I shrug.

He says, "You gonna be like that, it's gonna be a long day."

I want to tell him, "It's gonna be a long day any-way," but I just go, "Mm."

"Okay, I'll figure something out."

Pulling away from the curb, he clicks on the radio and the Stones are belting "Paint It Black." I love the Stones. I love this song. It's killing me not to sing along, but I don't want him to make fun of my singing or to think I'm having a good time.

Out of the corner of my eye, I notice a white graduation tassel hanging from the rearview. Under it, suction-cupped onto the dashboard, is this football guy bobblehead.

He notices me noticing. "That's Gerri's," he goes. "She's a big Buffalo Bills fan. Huge."

"Cool," I say, when it's anything but. I mean, how freakin' *uncool* is it to let your son know you've got a woman in your life—*other* than the woman you're *still legally married to*—by dropping her name like, *Oh yeah by the way that's GERRI's bobblehead you're lookin' at.*

I see him trying to decide whether to say anything else, but he turns up the volume instead and bops his head to the music. Now there are two bobbleheads in the car.

Just as the song ends, we pull into Betty & Pauls, this diner that's been around for, like, ever. (Addie has a cow that "Pauls" doesn't have an apostrophe. I tell her it's because Betty is married to two guys named Paul, so "Pauls" is a plural, not a possessive. She doesn't find this funny, although she is impressed that I stay awake in English class.) I hate saying it, but the shakes at Betty & Pauls are even better than the ones we make at the Candy Kitchen. I don't know what their secret is. And their pancakes? Their pancakes should be famous, like so famous you want to ask for their autograph before you eat them.

Addie in my head: *That is* so *not funny.*

Me in my head: *You're on vacation. Leave me alone. And FYI, asking pancakes for their autograph is funny.*

"You're having the pancakes, right?" my dad asks as if he's reading my mind. "Gotta have the pancakes. And how about a vanilla shake, Skeezo?"

"Nobody calls me Skeezo," I say.

"I do."

"Like I said."

Moving ahead of him toward the door of Betty & Pauls, I feel his hand grab my shoulder. "Hey!" he says sharply. I turn. His face is red.

"What?" I ask, all innocent, like I didn't just call him "nobody."

His nostrils flare as he takes in a deep breath. "Nothing," he says after a long exhale. "I just thought it was okay for me to call you Skeezo, like I used to. You're telling me it isn't. Got it. Let's move on."

also known as elvis

After we order our pancakes and vanilla shakes—
along with two orders of seasoned curly fries, which
if I ran the Candy Kitchen we would *so* have on the
menu—my dad starts asking me the usual questions.

1. How was school this year?
2. So what are you into?
3. What do you mean, nothing? Not fishing? You're not into fishing?
4. You got a girlfriend yet?

(I tell him "no comment" on that one, and then I
think, *Oh no, this is it! The Talk! The Man-to-Man Talk!*
But he doesn't go there. He asks another question.)

5. You still bowling?
6. No? When did you stop bowling?

(Uh, when I turned, like, nine.)

7. You follow any sports?
8. None?

9. You made any other guy friends besides
    Bobby and Joe?

(Okay, now I'm pretty sure he thinks I'm gay.
*No girlfriend. Doesn't like sports. 50 percent of his
guy friends are gay. He's got to be gay.* So I brace
myself a second time for The Talk. This should be
really good, him talking to me about s-e-x while
he's thinking I'm gay. Could be so entertaining
that maybe I'll let him believe it. But once again he
doesn't go there. He asks a question I should have
seen coming all along.)

10. So how do you think your mom is doing?

"Why don't you ask her?" I say.
"Because I'm asking you. Because I want to
know how *you* see her, Skeezo—sorry—*Skeezie.*"
Up until now I've been keeping my eyes looking
down at the menu, down at the table, down at the
pancakes, down at the fries, down at the shake, but
now I lift them up and look straight into his.

"She works two jobs," I tell him. "That's how I think she's doing."

"Yeah, that's hard," he goes, his voice all full of sympathy, even though his eyes don't blink.

I try to hold his stare, but before I know it my eyes are down again, looking at the crumbs stuck to the plate in the fake maple syrup like flies on fly-paper.

"She's tired all the time," I mumble.

"Yeah, I hate that. I hate that I haven't been able to help you guys out more. It's been tough finding work. But now that I have this new job and . . ."

And now instead of The Talk, I am getting The Pitch. The Sales Pitch. How he's become a responsible citizen, living in the Land of Opportunity (even though I heard in current events last year how half the major industry in Rochester has tanked) with *awesome* buddies who do *cool* stuff. Like he's got this one buddy (I wonder if he has any friends who are women or don't like being called buddy) who has this *sweet* cabin cruiser they take out fishing on the lake sometimes and this other buddy who's from New Orleans and is an *excellent* cook, who's teaching him how to make *amazing* stuff like Cajun deep-fried turkey and dirty rice.

"Sweet," I say.

"Awesome," I say.

"Excellent," I say.

And he just keeps going on and on, not hearing me, which isn't a totally bad deal because I sneak in an order for another vanilla shake and seasoned curly fries and he doesn't even notice. I'm not sure what he's getting at. Is he going to try to sell me a boat? Does he think I'll be impressed that he knows how to make dirty rice, whatever the heck that is? Will he ever mention Bobblehead Gerri?

None of the above. He winds it up with, "So I'm really going to try to do better for your mom and you guys. I know it's been tough. I mean, geez, here you are having to work at the Candy Kitchen, for cryin' out loud, and you're, what, twelve?"

"Thirteen," I say, "and I happen to like working at the Candy Kitchen."

"No, it's great," he goes, laying down some

bills on the table, including, I notice, a generous tip. "Free ice cream and all that."

"Yeah," I say. "Yeah, that's why I do it. Free ice cream."

Back in the car, I catch him glancing at his watch, like, *Okay, how many more hours do I have with the kid and what am I going to do with him?* Maybe that's not what he's thinking; maybe it's what I'm feeling about him, who knows. He starts up the engine, fastens his seat belt, then pulls out his phone and checks for messages.

Even with the AC on, I'm feeling the heat. I take off my jacket, ball it up in my lap, and wonder why I even wear it anymore. Why the hell I still care.

I Saw a Therapist Once for About Ten Minutes

Before I started wearing my dad's jacket, I looked like your basic nerd with bad-boy aspirations. I hunched up my shoulders and kept my head down and my hands shoved in my jeans pockets. My hair flopped in my face. I mumbled a lot.

What? What did you say?

That's what I heard all the time.

I *said*, I mumbled a lot. The only time I didn't mumble was when I wanted to get in a good wisecrack. Then I made sure I could be heard.

I acted tough, but that's all it was: an act. I didn't dress the part until my dad left and I found the one leather jacket he'd left behind hanging in the back of his and my mom's bedroom closet. I put it on right away, checked myself out in the mirror on the back of the closet door, and liked what I saw. After glopping up my hair with some mousse I found in the bathroom, I ran grooves through it with a comb so that I looked like I belonged in a street gang.

Okay, maybe a street gang from fifty years ago, but still . . .

My mom pretty much had a heart attack when she got home from work that night. "Go wash your hair!" she snapped. "And take that jacket off. We're throwing it out. You look like . . ."

She never finished her sentence, but I knew the end of it: BJ. *You look like BJ. You look like your dad.*

When I refused to take off the jacket or stop slicking back my hair, she threatened to:

1. ground me
2. take away my allowance
3. make me clean the cellar
4. make me live in the cellar
5. cut off my air supply

Nothing worked.

So one day she said, "I've made an appointment for you with Dr. Leslie, the therapist I've been seeing. He's been helping me and I think he can help you, too."

"Whatever," I mumbled.

"What? What did you say?"

Two days later I was sitting in a swivel chair across from this guy in a sweater-vest with a clipboard on his lap.

In my head I gave him props for the swivel chair. The sweater-vest and clipboard? No *way* was I talking to this dude.

I swiveled. He jabbered on about how my mom was concerned that I wouldn't take off the leather jacket and why wouldn't I take off the leather jacket and maybe I should stop swiveling now. I continued to swivel.

Finally he said, "Do you like to play chess?"

"Not really," I told him.

A big victory smile lit up his face. He got me to talk!

"Checkers?"

I shrugged.

We ended up playing checkers for the rest of the session. And the session after that. And the session after that. Once a week for forty-five minutes I played checkers with a middle-aged guy in a sweater-vest who let me win. How much was my mother paying for this?

I figured that playing checkers was better than swiveling to the point of getting dizzy or having to look past him at his stupid degrees hanging crooked on the wall or at his wife and kids laughing at me from their happy family photo-op photo from Disneyworld. *It's a small world after all, ha ha, splash splash.*

One time he noticed me glancing up at that picture, and that made him think it was okay to talk about families. Pretty soon I was talking about mine, and eventually he got me to tell him that I wore the jacket all the time because I thought maybe if I did, my dad would come back home. I don't know if I actually believed this or if I was saying it so he'd leave me alone.

"We call that magical thinking," he said, tapping his clipboard with his pen.

"Who's 'we'?" I mumbled.

"What?" he asked. "What did you say?"

I repeated myself in a slightly louder voice, just enough so he could hear me but not without having to lean forward and drop his clipboard on the floor.

"Let's keep the focus on you," he said, picking up his clipboard. I caught sight of a doodle of a duck before he returned the clipboard to his lap.

That was my last session with Dr. Leslie. He told my mother that she shouldn't worry, that I was just working through my grief over my dad's leaving, and that I'd stop wearing the jacket when I was ready.

He clapped me on the shoulder as we left his office. "I'm here for you if you need me," he said.

I wanted to tell him that I didn't need him; that I had friends to play checkers with who didn't charge by the hour. But I didn't say that. I could see in his face that he really wanted to help, and in a way he already had. He got my mom to back off and let me keep wearing my dad's jacket.

"Thanks," I told him in my loud wisecracking voice, even though this time I wasn't making a wisecrack. I was totally being sincere.

The Talk

"Whoa, check out that pooch!"

I have no idea what my dad is talking about. Pooch? Really? Who says pooch? All I know is that the Ranger has jerked to a halt, fast-forwarding me from my memories of Dr. Leslie and his swivel chair to the parking lot of Betty & Pauls, where my dad is pointing at something across the street.

"Huh?" I go.

"There, there!" he says, all excited.

When I follow the direction of his finger, I get excited, too.

"Holy tomato!" I say. I have no idea where this comes from.

Anyways, what I say isn't important. What I see is.

"That dog looks just like—"

"Penny!" my dad practically shouts. "I know, I know! It's amazing!"

"Do you think it *is* her? I mean, it could be, right?"

My dad burns rubber across the street without even looking both ways, which is bad. Lucky for us there are no other cars around. Pulling up alongside the girl who's walking the dog (Penny? our Penny?), he honks the horn and powers down the passenger window.

"Hey!" he calls out.

The girl turns and looks at us, a little scared. She's maybe eight or nine.

"Where'd you get your dog?" he goes.

"What?" she says. "Penny" pulls at the leash, eager to keep moving.

"Your dog is really cute," my dad says. "Just wondering where you got her."

"Him," the girl calls back. "He's a boy. We got him at the shelter."

"He's a boy?" I ask. How could Penny have turned into a boy?

"Uh-huh. His name is Oscar."

All of a sudden, Oscar stops looking like Penny.

He's smaller and his ears are too pointy. And he doesn't know who we are.

Not ready to give up, my dad asks, "How old is he?"

"He's two," the girl answers. "Um, I think I'd better go. My mom says I shouldn't—"

"Right. That's cool. It's just that, we like your dog, is all."

The girl breaks into a big smile. I remember smiling like that. It comes from knowing you have the best dog in the whole world and some stranger stopping to tell you that they see it, too.

After the girl and her dog walk away, I roll up my window and we just sit there for a few minutes, gazing out through the windshield, thinking about Penny.

"Remember the time she snuck up on the back porch and ate that stack of baloney sandwiches we'd set out?" my dad says with a chuckle. "Your mom was so pissed."

It comes back to me. "Yeah. We were going out to the lake to have a picnic for somebody's birthday."

"Uh-uh. It wasn't a birthday, it was just a Saturday. We did that a lot. Pack up some sandwiches, head out to the lake, and hang out for hours. Don't you remember that time you got sunburned so bad you wouldn't even let me carry you to the car?"

"No," I tell him, because I don't remember getting sunburned or my dad carrying me or not carrying me. I don't even remember going out to the lake on ordinary Saturdays. I thought it had to be for something special.

We're still looking out the windshield, keeping our eyes straight ahead. "It was best when we had Penny," my dad says, all quiet-like. "Tossing the Frisbee around for her to catch."

"Or throwing sticks into the water and watching her go after them and bring them back," I say. The times with Penny, those are easier to remember somehow.

My dad heaves a big sigh. "She was a great dog all right. I hate that she had to stay out back in that kennel all the time. She should have been in the house with her family, where she belonged. Hell, she could have had all the baloney sandwiches she wanted, if it was up to me."

We get quiet for a long time, just the sound of the AC keeping us company.

"I still can't figure how she got out of that kennel and ran off like she did," my dad says. My eyes fill up with tears, and I have to turn my head to the side window. No way can I let him see me like this. No way can I tell him what I know.

"Well, that's water under the bridge," he says, pulling slowly out onto the street. "It sure would have been nice if that was her today, though, wouldn't it, Skeezo? Sure would have been nice to see her again."

I nod my head so slightly it's like a mumble. As we drive along the familiar streets of Paintbrush Falls, the radio soft in the background, I'm surprised at how much I'm liking this. Him calling me Skeezo. Us talking about Penny. Just driving around together like we used to when I was a kid, the two of us, not knowing where we were going because where we were going wasn't the point. And then I start hating that these good feelings are slipping in through cracks I didn't even know were there. I don't *want* to like this. I don't want to like him.

After a while, he leans in and turns up the radio. "These guys are awesome," he says. "Listen to the drums. Man, if I could play like that . . ."

"You play drums?" I ask. First I heard.

"Yeah, look behind my seat," he says.

I do, and there's what looks like a snare drum.

"You in a marching band?"

He laughs. "Yeah, right. Me, in a marching band. That's a good one. No, I'm in a rock band. One of my buddies started it up a couple years back, and then about six months ago his drummer left town and—"

"Since when are you a drummer?" First he's wearing a tie, now he's a drummer. Seriously, who is this dude?

"I don't know. A year or two. It's something I always wanted to do, but who had the time or the money, and with three kids . . . not that I'm blaming you guys, it's just . . . I don't know. We got married so young, I never had a chance to do the stuff I wanted to. I had the Beast, sure, but your mom was always . . . no, I'm not going there. I don't blame her. It's just . . ."

He slaps his hand on the steering wheel and shakes his head. "It's just that I got this chance to play the drums and I'm doing it, man. That's all. I'm doing it. And hey, I'm not bad. Still learning, but getting better all the time."

"So where's the rest of the drum thingy?" I ask.

"Kit. It's called a kit. It's back home. I need to replace one of the nut boxes on the snare. That's why it's in the truck."

He looks over at me and we both crack up. I know we're thinking about what kind of joke we can make out of "nut boxes." I forgot that my dad and I think alike sometimes.

"I want to play the electric guitar," I tell him.

"Are you serious? That's what Gerri plays! She's in the band."

"Is that how you guys met?"

My dad sighs. "Your mom told you?"

"Yeah. So when were *you* going to tell me?"

"Sorry. I should have said something right off. It's hard, though, Skeeze. It's hard for me to tell you I'm marrying somebody else when your mom and I aren't even divorced yet. Life is strange, okay? I didn't see this coming. I mean, I knew it was no good between your mom and me. I knew there was no chance we'd get back together. But I was still kind of hoping we could be friends or something and I could be closer to you guys, spend more time together."

"If you didn't move so far away, we could've spent more time together," I say, but so soft I'm not sure he hears me.

We're pulled up at a red light now, and he turns to look at me.

"I miss our times together, kid. Look at you, you're stuck in a house with three girls. And hey, I like Gerri—I mean, I love Gerri. But it's not the same as . . . I miss my . . . you know what I'm trying to say here . . . I miss my son."

I have no clue what to say back. I don't even

have a clue what to feel. I wish the light would hurry up and change and he'd stop staring at me.

When it does, I breathe out and he changes the subject. "Hey, I got an idea! Let's go out to the music store at the mall. We can check out guitars. You want to?"

"Really?"

"Hell, yeah!"

"Okay. Sure."

He hangs a sharp right and we head out toward the mall. "There's this store in Rochester not far from where we live," he says. "They have *amazing* used guitars. We could get you a Fender Strat in good shape for maybe five, six hundred. What kind do you like?"

I wonder how he could come up with five or six hundred bucks to buy me a guitar when he can't even make support payments to my mom. But I shrug the thought off and tell him, "I've never even held one. How should I know?"

"Well, you will by the time we're done at the mall," he says, almost as excited now as when he thought he saw Penny. "I hope the store's still there. Hey, when you come to Rochester, I'll take you to Bernunzio's. You'll be blown away. And Gerri can give you some lessons. She's awesome. Wait'll you hear her sing. Oh, man."

"So that's how you met? The band?"

"Nah, we met at work . . . well, actually, we met at this bar . . . but it was hearing her sing and play that sealed the deal for me. Hey, there it is. Strings 'n' Things. It's still there. Pathetic name for a store, but they've got a big selection. Or at least they did. Del and I used to come here to mess around back in the day."

So my dad and I check out guitars for two whole hours that go by like they're fifteen minutes. I not only get to hold one, I get to try out a whole bunch of them. I even master a couple of power chord riffs, which is awesome. There's this one Yamaha I really like, and it's only a few hundred bucks. Yeah, I know: *only*. As if I could afford even that. But it's still a whole lot cheaper than that used Strat my dad was talking about.

The guy at the store says I'm a natural. I don't know if I should believe him or not since, hey, it's his job to sell guitars, right? But I think he figured out early on that we weren't buying, so who knows, maybe I really am a natural. All I know is I'm having a good time. And I keep right on having a good time through lunch at KFC and six games out at Spare Time Lanes.

After my dad drops me off at home ("See ya, Skeezo." "See ya, Dad."), I'm hardly through the door when my mom asks, "So did you two have your big man-to-man talk?"

It's the first time I've thought about it since this morning at Betty & Pauls. I'm not sure what to tell her. We never talked about sex or any stuff like that. We talked about missing Penny and playing drums and guitar. We ate fried chicken and bowled six games. And my dad said he missed his son.

"Yeah," I say. "Yeah, we did."

Can't Help Falling in Love

Here's something weird. With Sunday being so slow at the Candy Kitchen and then having Monday and Tuesday off, I find myself missing working there, and pretty soon I'm dreaming about making hot fudge sundaes and banana splits. In the dreams, I'm using these random ingredients, like ketchup and dog biscuits and nut boxes. Nut boxes! I don't even know what they are, but I'm topping off sundaes with them, and everybody seems to like them, because there's a big sign in the Candy Kitchen window (except it doesn't look anything like the Candy Kitchen, being a dream and all) that says SKEEZIE'S FAMOUS SUNDAES, NOW WITH NUT BOXES!

I wake up laughing. I swear, I'm so ready for my own reality show.

Anyways, Tuesday morning I walk Megan and Jessie to day camp (their third one this summer), then text Becca on the walk back home.

hey, we still got a date with a dog?

OMG! I AM SO PSYCHED! My mom says it's good ur coming with, so u can stop me from taking home every dog I see

who says I'm going to stop u?

lol!!! c u at 12

later

It's really peaceful when I get back home. No sisters. No mom. Then that dog Oscar pops into my head and I think: no dog.

I head out back to Penny's old doghouse. I'm all set to crawl inside when my phone buzzes in my jacket pocket.

You never call, you never write.

hi addie

You never capitalize, you never punctuate.

Hi! Addie?

That's better. How are you?

A.W,E:S?O;M-E!

I see that my being away hasn't robbed you of your sense of humor. What a shame. Miss me much?

Who is this again?

Very funny.

We go back and forth like this for a while, Addie eventually telling me what she's been doing with her grandma (who is cooler than 99 percent of the grandmothers on the planet) and me telling her what's been going on with me. When I say I'm looking at dogs with Becca in a couple of hours, she says, **Sounds like fun. Just be careful.**

what do you mean, I text back.

I wait a full minute until she writes, **Sorry, I've got to go. Getting our hands hennaed. Running late. Ciao.**

Okay:

1.   She has clearly been texting with Joe. Addie never said "ciao" before in her life.
2.   What does "getting our hands hennaed" mean?
3.   More important, what does "just be careful" mean? Careful of what?

Becca and her mom show up early. I've met her mom before. She's pretty nice as moms go. And she seems even nicer today because she's as excited about getting a dog as Becca is. In the back of her station wagon are a crate, a doggy bed, and two overstuffed, humongous bags full of toys and food from Pete's Pets.

"I guess you're planning on going home with a dog," I crack, and they both smile at me from the front seat.

"Thanks so much for going with us, Skeezie," says Mrs. Wrightsman. "I'm afraid we *both* need somebody to be the voice of reason."

"I'm not sure I'm the right guy for the job," I say. "I'm a sucker for dogs."

"I was telling Mom about Penny," says Becca, turning down the corners of her mouth into an *aw, poor Skeezie* frown. I *think* she means it.

"I'm so sorry," Mrs. Wrightsman says. "I know it happened a long time ago, but I don't believe we ever get over losing a pet. I had a canary named Alice that flew out of the window when I was, oh, nine or so. And to this day—"

"Mom!" Becca says sharply. "I don't think a canary and a dog are the same thing."

"Well, of course they're not the same thing, Becca. One is a bird and one is a dog. But you didn't know Alice, did you? I did, and let me tell you, she was not your usual canary."

"Omigod!" Becca cries. "I *so* have to tweet that!"

While Becca's thumbs are busy tweeting "She was not your usual canary," her mom and I exchange sympathetic looks in the rearview mirror.

"I get what you're saying, Mrs. Wrightsman," I tell her.

"I know you do, Skeezie. And please call me Lainy."

"Um, okay." Like that is ever going to happen.

Becca looks up from her phone and squeals, "Omigod, we're here, we're here! Mom, pull in, hurry up!"

"Becca, calm down! Do you want me to have an accident?"

Becca clamps her lips tight and keeps squealing in this muffled sort of way. I can't decide if I think she's way cute or obnoxious—like Megan, four years older.

After Mrs. Wrightsman, a.k.a. Lainy, parks, we run to the door of the shelter, Becca practically tearing my arm off. Inside there's another family, already looking at dogs.

Becca says in a stage whisper, "This isn't fair! What if they find the dog *I* want before I've even *met* her? Or him."

"What if the dog you want was adopted yesterday?" I stage-whisper back.

Becca's mom comes up behind us. "*Thank* you, Skeezie. You see? You *are* the voice of reason."

I puff up just a little imagining that Mrs. Wrightsman sees me as good son-in-law material, then think how weird I'm getting.

It isn't long before we're following behind the other family. They are totally Nick at Nite: blond mom; slightly balding dad wearing glasses; teenage boy in sagging pants, showing off his boxers; preteen girl in short shorts and flip-flops, her hair pulled back in a ponytail. All that's missing to make them the perfect family is a dog, and that's about to be remedied. We're walking down a corridor of cages where Becca is melting and cooing and going ballistic over every single dog, even the ones that look like they want to rip you apart just for fun.

"Ooh, what about this one?" she asks, dropping to her knees and coming face-to-face with a mutt that could be a cross between a poodle, a terrier, and a mop.

"Her name is Trixie Belle," she says.

"Pretty cute," I go. "The dog, not the name."

"I agree on both counts," says her mom, "but we could always change her name. Should we ask to take her out into the play yard?"

Becca nods, then turns her head and gasps.

"Omigod!" she cries.

The boy in the almost-perfect family is holding the perfect puppy. Trixie Belle is history.

"They're taking *my* dog!" Becca goes in this pained voice, like her whole world has collapsed. "Look at it, look at it! It's the most adorable thing *ever*! We can't let them take it!"

Okay, this is one seriously cute puppy. I know,

I know: all puppies are seriously cute. But this one is like award-winning seriously cute. It's all shaggy fur and big ears and wiggly bottom. And with its round belly and black-and-white coloring it looks as much like a panda as a puppy—at least, from where we're standing.

Becca says, "I'm going over there."

"Becca," her mother warns.

"I'm not going to *do* anything, I'm just going to say hi."

Watching her daughter walk off, Mrs. Wrightsman rolls her eyes, sighs, and says, "Whatever Becca wants, Becca gets."

I nod my head like I get what she's talking about, and we start to follow after Becca—and that's when I take a turn into a completely different story. All of a sudden, I'm no longer there with Becca, her mother, the puppy, or Mr. and Mrs. Nick at Nite and their almost-perfect kids. All of a sudden, I only have eyes for Licky.

Okay, Licky is, like, the worst name ever. Even worse than Trixie Belle.

But next to Penny, Licky is the best dog ever. Trust me, I can tell.

She is looking up at me from her cage. I mean, right at me. It's like we *know* each other. I almost think it *is* Penny, because it's that kind of knowing. But she looks nothing like Penny. She's got short hair, for one thing. She looks like a butterscotch sundae, white with big caramel-brown splotches, but a sundae with floppy ears and a hound-dog face. She ain't nothin' but a hound dog, and oh man, those eyes. They're brown, like mine, and all happy and sad at the same time. And I swear, after we've been staring at each other for all of twenty seconds, her mouth breaks into a big smile and she hangs out her tongue like it's a flag with some kind of message written on it. Which of course it has.

I'm yours, it says. *Take me home.*

I drop down and press my nose to the chain link. Licky presses her nose to mine. It's like Penny all over again. And then I start doing this completely crazy thing, as if there's nobody else in the room, which as far as Licky and I are concerned, is true.

So what is this crazy thing I do? I sing to her. The King, of course. But not "Hound Dog," which is probably what you're guessing. No, I sing, "Can't Help Falling in Love."

I haven't even finished the part about the river flowing surely to the sea when Licky starts licking. It's not the easiest thing to sing to a dog when she's got her tongue all over your face; but when you're singing Elvis, anything is possible.

"Would you like to take her out to the play yard?" I hear someone ask.

I look up, and there's this woman probably my grandma's age, bending over. She's wearing a smock kind of thing, which I'm pretty sure means she works here, or volunteers, or whatever. She has caught me in the act of singing to a dog, but she doesn't look like she thinks there's anything strange about it. She acts like people come in here all the time and sing to dogs. And maybe they do.

"Um, no," I say to her. "I—I'm just here with my friend, uh—she's the one getting a dog. I'm just here to lick. I mean, look."

She laughs. "Are you sure you don't want to take her out and run around with her? She could use the exercise; you'd be doing me a favor."

I come this close to saying yes. In fact, it takes everything in me *not* to say yes. But I shake my head no.

"Okay," the woman says. "But if you change your mind, come find me and I'll let her out. My name's Peg. Okay?"

I nod. "Okay."

When I turn back, Licky is staring right at me, her big smiley mouth still open, full of dopey happiness and hope.

"I hate to break it to you," I tell her, "but life sucks." She probably knows this already. Her life brought her to this shelter, after all. But I can't help saying what I feel, and what I feel right now is that life sucks, big-time. I want to take her home with all my heart, but there's no way. Instead, I have to go back to the other story—the one with Becca and the puppy she is now holding in her arms, the puppy that is licking *her* face.

"Goodbye, Licky," I say. "I hope somebody nice takes you home."

"Omigod, Skeezie!" Becca says when I join them. "You're not going to *believe* it! There are *two* puppies! They're brothers. Cody is taking Charlie and I'm taking Max."

"Who's Cody?" I ask, with the tiny piece of my brain that even cares.

"I'm Cody," says the guy with the low-riding pants. He's holding the other puppy—Charlie, I guess—which means that Becca has managed to end up with just the puppy she wanted. How does it not surprise me that her mom was right?

"And guess what! This is *so* awesome. Omigod!" Becca gushes. "Cody lives near us, so we're going to have playdates for the puppies! Right, Cody?"

Is she batting her eyelashes at him? I mean, who does that in real life?

"Truth," Cody says. And who says *that* in real life?

"What do you say, Skeezie?" Mrs. Wrightsman

asks, appearing over my shoulder. "Don't you think Max is the perfect dog for us?"

"Sure," I go, as if I'm some sort of dog and family matchmaker. I have no idea if Max is the perfect dog for Becca and her mom. All I know is that Licky is the perfect dog for me, and as my grandma would say, "That and a buck fifty will buy you a cup of coffee."

"Ooh, ooh, let's take the boys out to the play yard," Becca says.

"Sweet," says Cody, turning to his sister. "Cat, you coming?"

His sister's name is Cat. Seriously.

The adults go off in the direction of the office to do the paperwork. Becca, Cody, Cat, and their matching perfect dogs go off in the direction of the play yard. And I stand there, caught between two stories, the one where Becca doesn't say, *Skeezie, you coming?* and the one where I can't stop hearing Licky say, *I'm yours.*

Back at Becca's, we're having pizza and playing with Max when Becca's phone rings. She's so happy to hear from whoever it is that she runs out of the room, going, "I know, I know, aren't they so cute?" leaving me to hang out with Max. I'll admit it, he's a whole lot of fun, chasing after the rope toy I toss him, then running back and playing tug-of-war. But my mind is on Licky.

I've got to tell somebody about her. I reach for my phone and start to punch in Joe's number, then stop and consider texting Addie. But it's not really either of them I want to tell. It doesn't make any sense, but I punch in the number I've been trying to forget for two years. On the third ring, he picks up.

"Hey, Dad," I say. "I met this great dog at the shelter today."

The Skeezie-Steffi Dialogues: Dads

Skeezie: I just don't get what the stinkin' deal is.

Steffi: I know, right? One minute you hate them, the next minute you miss them, then you love them, then you hate them again.

Skeezie: Yeah, and you forget all the good parts. Now he's back and I'm remembering stuff I'm not sure I even want to remember. How much fun we had sometimes. How we'd think the same thing at the same time and look at each other like we totally get it. That's something I never have with my mom.

Steffi: My dad left four years ago. We had all these little in-jokes and secret codes between us.

Skeezie: Do you still see him?

Steffi: Oh, yeah. A lot, actually. But it's not the same. Once he left he was too busy having in-jokes and secret codes with his girlfriend to have them with me anymore.

Skeezie: That why he left? He had a girlfriend?

Steffi: Mm-hmm. He sat my brother and me down—Will was twelve—and cried the whole time he told us. I'd never seen my dad cry before. I couldn't believe the first time wasn't because somebody had died, but because he was telling us goodbye.

Skeezie: It *feels* like somebody dying.

Steffi: Tell me. I could hardly breathe. It's like time stopped and I kept waiting for it to go back to before. I don't think I said anything, just sat there trying to make sense of it. I felt like I was going to throw up.

Skeezie: Did he tell you about the girlfriend?

Steffi: Not right away. Did yours?

Skeezie: I don't think there was a girlfriend. Who knows? There is now. Anyways, you're

	lucky your dad told you he was leaving, even if he was crying.
Steffi:	Your dad didn't tell you?
Skeezie:	My sisters, but not me.
Steffi:	That's awful.
Skeezie:	Yeah.
Steffi:	What happened? You don't have to tell me if you don't want to.
Skeezie:	It's okay, I want to. So, they'd been fighting a lot, and they were having this one real blowout. He'd been looking for work and the only job he could find was at McDonald's, and he wouldn't take it because he said he was better than that. My mom was cursing him out something bad. They didn't know I was in the next room. Or they didn't care. Megan and Jessie were out front playing. Anyways, my dad said that my mom and us would be better off without him, and he'd be better off without us. He said he was leaving to get a decent job and he'd send money.

Steffi: What did your mom say?

Skeezie: She told him if he was going, he should pack his stuff and get the hell out. So he went to pack and I went to hide in this crawl space we have under the house. I watched him loading his stuff on the Harley, then walk back and bend down to where my sisters were playing. I couldn't hear what they said. Megan told me later he told them he was going away for a while to look for work. He wouldn't say when he was coming back. I waited for him to try to find me, but he just stood up and squinted back at the house for a few minutes. Then he revved up his bike and drove away.

Steffi: Did he at least call you later?

Skeezie: Two weeks later. But I wouldn't talk to him. I couldn't stop thinking how he'd said he'd be better off without us. And how he never looked for me to say goodbye.

Steffi: Maybe it was too hard for him.

Skeezie: Hey, too bad. He never did the hard stuff anyway. I held Jessie's head for two hours while she threw up the other night. My dad never held my head once.

Steffi: And then . . .

Skeezie: And then they come back and ride you around in their pickup trucks and take you bowling and looking at guitars. And you can't help it: It feels good.

Steffi: What kind of stinkin' deal is that, right?

Skeezie: (laughing) Hate 'em, love 'em, miss 'em, hate 'em, love 'em, miss 'em. *That* is the stinkin' deal, my friend. That's the stinkin' deal.

If I Live to Be a Hundred, I Want to Be Mrs. Miller

Over the next couple of days, my mom takes mornings off work so she and my dad can meet with a lawyer and get their divorce settled. Thursday morning it rains. Again. Jessie and Megan say that they shouldn't have to go to day camp, and my mom's so tired of fighting them over "nickels and dimes," as she puts it, that she caves and says they can stay home. Guess who doesn't have to work that morning and gets to stay home with them.

I'm starting to wish my job at the Candy Kitchen was full-time. Every day. Seriously.

I decide that if I'm going to get stuck baby-sitting Megan and Jessie for four hours when I wasn't planning on it, at least I'm going to have some fun. So I make us waffles and coffee for breakfast and use up all the bacon. And then we bake cookies together, except we use M&M's instead of chocolate chips, and the colors run so that Jessie says they look like they're finger-painted.

So then we finger-paint.

It ends up that we have a good time, and for once Megan stops being a snark monster and actually resembles a human being.

When my mom comes through the door around noon, she finds us laughing over a contest of who can make the loudest and most convincing fart noises with their armpits. She doesn't ask why we all have our shirts hiked up over one shoulder. She doesn't say, "How nice to come home to the sound of laughter." She doesn't even look at us. She heads straight to her bedroom and announces, "I'm going to work."

"Well, hi there to you, too," I say. "And by the way, I also have to go to work."

"I am aware of that, Schuyler," she says in a voice that dares me to talk back one more time. "Megan and Jessie, you're spending the afternoon with your father. He's waiting outside. Skeezie, he wants to talk to you."

And *slam* goes the bedroom door.

"Are Mommy and Daddy divorced now?" Jessie asks.

The rain has stopped. My dad is leaning against the Ranger where it's parked at the curb, arms crossed over his chest, boots crossed at the ankles. He's wearing the same button-down shirt and tie he wore when he came to town last Friday, only now they're both wrinkled.

We nod our heads at each other, the way guys do, with our mouths tight and our eyes down. My hands are shoved in the pockets of my shorts, and I'm trying to think of something to say. Seems like he is, too.

Finally he goes, "What's up?"

"Megan and Jessie'll be out in a minute," I tell him. "They're getting their girl stuff together."

He nods, then turns and spits.

"You and Mom okay?" I ask.

This gets him to look at me, and he looks at me like I'm nuts. "We're hashing out a divorce. 'Okay' isn't maybe the word. Listen, you want to bowl a couple games and have us some supper tonight? I'll drop the girls off at Aunt Lindsay's, then swing by the Candy Kitchen and pick you up a little after five. That when you get off work?"

"Yeah," I tell him. "But I was thinking about going over to Zachary's. He's got this new game he wants—"

"Fine, whatever," my dad goes. "I've got stuff I can do with Del. No biggie."

"No, I can change it. I mean, it wasn't definite or anything. Maybe we could mess around with some guitars again."

"Who, you and me and Del?"

"No, you and me. Wasn't that what you were saying?"

He spits again and says, "Yeah, yeah. That's what I was saying. My head's screwy right now. So I'm picking you up a little after five?"

I nod and say sure. "You going to be wearing that tie?" I ask him, expecting him to laugh.

He doesn't. He just kicks at the grass and looks past me at the house.

"Why do girls have to take forever?" he says. "Huh? Why do they always got to fuss and bother about everything? You're always *waiting* on them. What are they *doing* in there?"

"It's girl stuff, Dad. Like I said. They'll be out in a minute."

He kicks at the grass again. "Why do they have to make everything so hard? Complicate everything. Why's that, huh? You got an answer for me, Skeezo? You're an expert on girls, aren't you? Living with three of them. What's the answer?"

I shrug and mumble. I don't think he's talking about Megan and Jessie anymore, and even if he were, I wouldn't have an answer for him.

"Girls are a mystery," is the best I can come up with.

He nods his head and says, "You got that right."

*   *   *

The afternoon goes kind of slowly. Donny teaches me how to use the deep fryer, which is cool, except for how it reminds me of when Kevin made a joke about my dipping my hair in the oil. Kevin is about as funny as a funeral. But I don't know that it's humor he's really going for.

Anyways, I make myself a big order of sweet potato fries for lunch, and then, in between waiting on customers, Steffi and I come up with a list of songs we'd have on the jukebox if we owned the place. Because if we owned the place, you'd better believe we'd bring back the jukebox.

When it's my turn and I say, "Crazy," by Patsy Cline, Steffi goes, "Aha!"

"Don't get your panty hose in a twist," I tell her. "I don't like that song any more than I did the first time I heard it. I'm putting it on the list because *you* like it."

"Well, aren't you a gentleman," she says.

I bow and tell her, "Well, I guess I rightly am."

She then throws a dirty, wet rag at me. "Although," she says, "I don't know that a gentleman would tell a lady not to get her panty hose in a twist."

Throwing the rag right back at her, I go, "Who said anything about a lady?"

Steffi dodges the rag and it flies past her to land at the feet of Mrs. Miller, the only customer at the moment. Mrs. Miller is about a hundred years old. She comes in every afternoon right at three for a bowl of chocolate ice cream with whipped cream on top. It takes her about a half hour to eat the bowl of ice cream, because she says, every time we put it down in front of her, "I intend to savor every bite."

"Mrs. Miller!" I go, running to pick up the rag. "Sorry about that."

Mrs. Miller doesn't speak until the spoonful of ice cream she's just put in her mouth dissolves. "No harm done," she says, wiping her mouth as she does after each bite. "You young people are a barrel of monkeys. You're my entertainment."

What can I say? You've got to love Mrs. Miller.

By the time five o'clock rolls around, Steffi and I

have wiped down every surface at least three times; filled every salt and pepper shaker, every ketchup bottle, every napkin holder; washed out every rag; and come up with a list of 127 songs we'd have on our jukebox. It's been such a slow day, Donny tells me to take tomorrow off and just come in for a few hours on Saturday.

Steffi finds Mrs. Miller's glasses on the seat of the booth where she was sitting and says she'll take them to her, because Mrs. Miller lives just a few buildings down, in an apartment over the hardware store.

"It always smells like sawdust and soup," Steffi tells me as if she's taken Mrs. Miller's left-behind things to her more than a few times.

"Sawdust and soup, sawdust and soup," I belt out in my best Patsy Whiny voice, "I got my mem'ries o' sawdust and soup!"

That's when my dad walks in.

"Forget the electric guitar," he goes. "What you need is a banjo, boy. Yee-haw!"

"Banjo Boy!" Steffi calls me, which gets her and

my dad laughing. Then she stops cold, catching herself, because this is my dad, after all.

"The stinkin' deal," I say to her.

Nodding, she turns to wipe down the counter a fourth time as my dad swings his arm around my shoulders and we head out the door.

Surprises Come Flying Faster Than Twizzlers

My dad's game sucks. Usually, he bowls in the 200s. Tonight, his middle name could be Gutter Ball.

Joe, talking to me in my head: *That's two names.*

Me, talking to Joe in my head: *It's two* words. *Now get out of my head.*

In the real world, I say, "Dad, you feelin' all right?"

He just grunts and mumbles something about having things on his mind.

Halfway through the second game he says, "Let's get out of here, Skeezo. Want to go take another look at that Yamaha?"

"Sure!" I say, even though it means leaving in the middle of whupping my dad's butt.

On the way over to the mall, we stop for gas.

"You fill it up," he tells me, tossing me his credit card. "I gotta run inside for a minute. You want anything?"

"No, thanks."

Standing here pumping gas, I bop my head to the chord progression I learned the other day. I can't help wondering if my dad is maybe going to buy that Yamaha for me. To get my mind off something I both want (the guitar) and am not so sure I want (my dad being the one to get it for me), I think how cool I must look with my greased-back hair and my black leather jacket, bopping my head to guitar riffs, pumping gas into a banged-up pickup truck. I am one cool dude. Just to look even cooler, I spit. *So* cool. I spit again. This time all that comes out is a pathetic *ppppt* noise and a dribble of saliva on my chin. It's amazing how fast you can go from hoping everybody's checking you out to praying to be invisible.

I'm wiping off the spit with my jacket sleeve when I notice my dad inside the gas station, talking on his phone. He's pacing back and forth, chopping the air with his left hand like he's making points or something. Maybe he's talking to his lawyer. Maybe my mom.

Back in the truck I get restless waiting for him. Before I know it, I'm poking around the glove compartment. Glove compartments are like umbrella stands. Who uses them for gloves? Who *wears* gloves, except in the winter, when the only time you'd put them in a *compartment* (weird word) would be after you were wearing them outside and they're all packed with frozen chunks of ice and snow? And then they'd melt all over everything and . . .

This is how my mind works when it's restless.

After pushing aside a bunch of papers, I spot a photograph. I pull it out and there's my dad standing with his arm around a woman. A really pretty woman, with lots of curly blond hair and big earrings and lips. She's got on a fuzzy pink turtleneck sweater, but even so you can see she's got . . . well, she's got curves in the right places, as my grandpa used to say right before my grandma would hit him and tell him he was disgusting. My dad has this woman pressed up tight against him and you can tell there's nowhere else she wants to be; they're both looking right at the camera, smiling the kind of happy, proud smile that that girl walking Oscar had when we told her we liked her dog.

No question. This is Gerri.

I get a kind of sick feeling in the pit of the stomach, and right away I know why: I never once saw my dad look this happy in any of the pictures he was in with my mom. I never saw him this relaxed. With my mom, he always looked like he was half there and half somewhere else. Kind of the way he looked when he was bowling tonight.

I go back to nosing around the glove compartment, telling myself I'm not looking for anything in particular and knowing that's a lie. A picture of us—me and Megan and Jessie, our mom and our dad—that's what I'm looking for. That's what I want to believe he keeps in his glove compartment. A picture of his family, right in there next to the one with Gerri. But big surprise. I come up empty-handed.

Or almost empty-handed. I do find the registration for the Ranger. It's in Gerri's name. This isn't my dad's truck. It's not even his glove compartment.

"Got you something," I hear, as a package of Twizzlers comes flying in through the open driver's-side window. I click the glove compartment closed as quietly as I can and stick the photo of Gerri and my dad in the inside pocket of my jacket.

"Long time in the john," I say, ripping open the Twizzlers.

"I had to make a phone call," he says. "Thanks for getting the gas."

"No worries," I tell him.

"Ha! That's a good one. No worries. Good luck with life, pal."

He grabs a Twizzler, sticks an end of it in his mouth, and says, "Let's go eat. Then I'll drive you home."

So much for the Yamaha.

I convince him to go to the food court at the mall, figuring that maybe after we eat he'll be in a better mood and I can steer him over to Strings 'n' Things.

We're sitting there halfway through our pizza when I hear, "Oh, my goodness, it's Skeezie!"

There is only one person I know who says, "Oh, my goodness."

"Hey, Zachary!" I call out.

Zachary and Kelsey are waving from the fountain in the center of the food court. They look like a couple, except they're not because:

1. Kelsey is Bobby's girlfriend.
2. Zachary was voted Most Likely to Be Gay Even If He Doesn't Know It by pretty much everybody who's ever met him.

"Who's that?" Dad asks as they start coming over.

"Friends from school," I say. "Kelsey and Zachary."

"*That's* who you were going to play video games with tonight?" he asks. I can see his face register the fact that Zachary, in his Hawaiian shirt and I LOVE GYMNASTICS baseball cap, is my only other guy friend besides Bobby and Joe. Put another check in the MY SON IS GAY column.

When I introduce them, Zachary goes, "I can't *believe* you're Skeezie's father. You look so young."

"Uh, yeah," says my dad, who probably thinks it's beyond weird that one of my "buddies" would compliment him on his looks.

I ask Kelsey if she's heard from Bobby, and she shakes her head no.

"I can't wait for him to come home. Just two more days," she says, crossing her fingers like that's going to make the time go by faster.

Zachary starts talking about this movie they just saw and the stuff they bought at the dollar store after the movie and how they're meeting up with Kelsey's parents over at the new Chinese restaurant at the other end of the mall, and I catch my dad texting under the table.

"Now, son," I say in this deep, stern voice, "I thought we agreed you weren't going to text during meals."

Zachary guffaws in this totally doofus way he

has, and my dad looks at both of us like we're from another planet.

"I'll be back," he says, and heads off toward the men's room.

No sooner is he out of sight than I hear another voice call my name. But this one isn't saying, "Oh, my goodness."

"Yo, Tookis! What're you doin'? Stealin' Joey's boyfriend?"

Kevin Hennessey is heading right toward us; his big brother Cole is with him. If you think Kevin is trouble, let me tell you: Cole is a disaster.

"Nice hat there, Faggory," Kevin says. "Pays to advertise."

Kevin is of the belief that only gay guys are into gymnastics.

If Kevin always has a smirk on his face (and he does), Cole looks like he could be one of those dogs out at the shelter that are just salivating to rip you apart.

I'm not sure where I get the nerve, but I look Kevin right in his smirking face and say, "How are things at St. Andrew's? They teach you any-thing about human kindness yet?" Both Kevin and Cole were pulled out of public school this year. Let's just say they weren't known for their polite behavior.

"Don't be a fag," Cole goes.

"Too late for that!" Kevin cracks.

"Nice talk for a couple of Catholic schoolboys," I say.

That's all it takes. Cole steps forward and shoves me. "You insulting my religion, fag?" he snarls.

I know enough not to shove back. I stand there holding his stare, just hoping he can't see that I'm one heartbeat away from peeing my pants.

"Um, I think maybe we should be going," Zachary says quietly. "I mean, we're supposed to be meeting Kelsey's parents."

If Zachary was hoping to slip away unnoticed, it's not working. Cole turns and grabs him. "Aww, ain't that sweet? 'We're supposed to be meeting Kelsey's parents.' What're you two, gettin' married? I don't think they're going to like it, their daughter marrying a faggot."

If I thought I was going to pee my pants a minute ago, Zachary looks like he is going to pass right out. His face has turned white. I can't see Kelsey, but I can hear her next to me, making these little whimpery noises in her throat. I know I should do something, but I can't move. The worst thing is, and I hate myself for saying it, but I'm glad the attention is on Zachary and not me.

Cole must be reading my mind, because he says, "Don't think I've forgotten about you, faggot."

"Who you calling faggot?"

No, that's not me finding my courage. That's my dad, who's suddenly on the scene, grabbing Cole by the shoulder and swinging him around so they're face-to-face.

"You calling my son a faggot? You call anybody a faggot, maybe you should start by lookin' in the mirror!"

Cole shoves my dad now. Hard. "Bring it on, old man!" he goes.

My dad regains his balance and shoves back. "You want a fight, boy? I'll give you a fight!"

"Dad!" I shout. "Don't hit him! He's a kid. You could get arrested."

"Who made you such a Goody Two-shoes?" my dad says, his face all red and puffy with anger. "Come on, Skeezo, defend your friend. Defend yourself! Or let me do it! Jerks like this, you got to stand up to them or they'll run all over you!"

While my dad's distracted talking to me, Cole swings. My dad ducks and comes back, ready with a swing of his own. But before he can deliver it, we hear a whistle and a security cop shouting, "Break it up! Stop it right now or I'll take you both in!"

I shut out the whole blame game that follows. I just want to get out of here as fast I can. Away from my friends seeing my dad act the way he did. Away from them knowing he acted the way he did because I'm a loser who backs down the minute things get scary. Away from Kevin and Cole, who acted the way they did because they are sick with hate and I don't get that and never will.

194

I'm a long way from the cool dude who was pumping gas just an hour ago.

My dad and I ride home in silence.

A million things are going through my brain. But the one that keeps beating out all the others is the thought that he's ashamed of me for not fighting back.

When we pull up in front of the house, he cuts the engine. Clearing his throat, he says, "Listen, Skeezie, maybe it's not the best time . . . or maybe it is, I dunno . . . but there's something I've been wanting to say to you. It's been on my mind all night."

"Is this 'the talk,' Dad?" I go. "You gonna tell me how to be a man? *Fight* like a man? Be tough?"

He reaches over and lays his hand on my shoulder. "What are you talking about? No. It's nothing like that. What I did back there, that was stupid. Are you kidding me? That's not standing up for yourself. That's laying yourself down in the gutter with the other bums. And I shouldn't have used that word. Just because he did, that's no excuse. That was disrespecting you and your friends. No, that's not what I want to talk to you about."

He takes a deep breath and keeps his hand steady on my shoulder.

"What it is, is . . . I want you to come live with me, son. With Gerri and me. We both want you to. I told your mom this morning, and she says it's up to you. So think about it, will you? You don't have to answer me right now. Just think about it. That's all I'm asking."

Fifteen Minutes

In an instant I go from total shock to wanting to kill my mom.

Harsh? Ya think?

But whoa, I mean, dude, one minute my mom needs me for everything from feeding her daughters to fixing the toilet, and the next minute it's, see ya, sayonara, ciao kiddo, go live with your dad. If ever there was a serious "what's up," this is it.

I shrug my dad's hand off my shoulder and exit the Ranger as fast as I can.

"I'll call you tomorrow!" he calls after me.

Whatever.

From the sidewalk I can hear my mom inside the house yelling at Megan to stop watching TV and get to bed. This must wake Jessie up, because she's suddenly crying and my mom is screaming, "Now what!" And this makes Jessie cry louder and Megan turn up the volume of the

TV, and this insane laugh track turns the whole house into a sitcom.

I need to change the channel.

Inside Penny's old doghouse I try to make sense of my crazy life. Once upon a time, I must have been a happy baby and my mom and dad must have been happy parents. Right? I mean, even if it wasn't for long, there must have been a time when they were all *goo-goo* and *ga-ga* and *kitchy-kitchy-koo* whenever they saw me. Tickled my feet and made me laugh. Rubbed their faces in my belly and sang little songs about their sweet baby boy.

Kelsey was telling me once about this artist named Andy Warhol who said that in the future everybody would be famous for fifteen minutes. He must have said this a long time ago, because when you look at reality shows and YouTube and stuff like that, it's true. The future he was talking about is now.

So isn't it like that when you're born? Don't you get at least fifteen minutes of being famous to your parents? Of being the center of their universe? Of being loved without anybody yelling or crying or leaving?

How come it falls apart? Steffi's dad left. Becca's dad left. My dad left. And now my mom couldn't care less if I leave.

Maybe I should.

I pull the picture of my dad and Gerri out of my pocket. There's enough light coming through the cracks in the broken boards that I can just make it out. All I see when I look at them is that they're happy. If I live with them, maybe I'll be happy, too. Maybe my mom knows that. Maybe she's saying I'll be better off without her and Megan and Jessie.

Maybe she's saying they'll be better off without me.

I'm so tired I can't even move. I fall asleep holding that photo, my head resting against the splintery inside of Penny's doghouse.

Sometime later, I feel my mom's hands on my arms.

"Come inside," she says. "Come to bed."

Confusion Balls Exploding

The next morning I wake up to find a note on the table by my bed. It's lying on top of the picture of Dad and Gerri.

"Hi, baby," it starts. (Three guesses who it's from.) "I've taken the girls to camp. Kyra's mom is going to pick them up after for a playdate. You're off duty for the day! Your dad is coming by at twelve to take you to lunch. I couldn't remember if you have to work. If you do, let him know.

"Love you, Mom.

"P.S. I bet you thought I didn't know about your hideout. I'm glad I did."

Rubbing my head (confusion balls exploding in my brain), I put the note back on the table and reach for the *Get Fuzzy* desk calendar Addie gave me after she and DuShawn broke up. Tomorrow is Saturday. My friends will be coming home. The first thing I'll want to do is walk over to Bobby's house.

He's the best person I can think of to help me figure this whole mess out.

But my dad might expect an answer before tomorrow. I'd text Addie or Joe, but it's still early, and they're on their last day of their vacations, and why ruin it for them? Besides, sometimes you really want to talk to somebody face-to-face. I could talk to Steffi, but then I come up with the crazy idea of biking out to Becca's house. Maybe it's not crazy, but it feels that way because I've never really talked to Becca about anything serious, other than Penny. I sure never asked her for advice. But hey, she's been through this whole divorce thing, and she lives with her mom and stepdad. So I convince myself that the idea is not crazy. I decide, as Addie would put it, that it's brilliant.

Turns out it's neither crazy nor brilliant. It's just bad.

Before she moved away, Becca lived right here in the village, just down the street from Addie. When they came back, her family moved into Graymoor Estates, this development a couple of miles out of town where if you squint the houses all look the same: big and puffed up, like SUVs or those fuzzy boots the girls all wear. It's not like they're mansions or anything, but they're a whole lot nicer than any of the houses me and my other friends live in. And the streets have names like Willow Way and Warblers Lane. They're big on *W*s. Becca lives at 25 Windswept Court.

I text her to ask if it's okay for me to come and she says, **awesome.** Lowercase. No exclamation point. But still: *awesome.* So after a bowl of this weird health store version of Cheerios my mom gets (once a month she tries to get us to eat healthy), I pump some air in my tires and head off.

Graymoor Estates, here I come.

When I pull up in front of her house, Becca is lying out on a towel, working on a tan. You would think the first thing I would notice is that she's wearing a bikini top and short shorts, but instead I'm scanning the towel for sunblock. I don't see any.

"You never heard of ultraviolet rays?" I say,

dropping my bike. "You want to get skin cancer?"

If I could, I'd hit delete. But I've already hit send. It's confirmed: Like Buddy the Elf in that old Christmas movie, I am a Cotton-Headed Ninny Muggins.

"Wow," she says. "Thanks, Mom."

"Sorry. I just . . . you know, you don't want to get . . ."

"Skin cancer. Right."

"Um, nice top," I go, neatly moving the focus away from death-causing skin lesions to her breastal region. Nice move, Muggins.

"Wow," Becca says again, this time meaning it and sitting up to give me a better look. "Thanks! I just bought it. It's JC Penney, but don't tell anybody."

I zip my lips, then say, "Where's Max?"

Wrapping her arms around her legs, Becca rests her head on her knees. "Over at Cody's," she tells me. "He's having a playdate with Charlie. It's hot out here. You want a Diet Coke?"

"Sure."

For the next twenty minutes or so, it goes on like this, easy talk and Diet Cokes in Becca's kitchen, which looks like something on HGTV. In my head, I'm thinking how it's not so hard talking to girls, after all. I guess it's a skill I picked up this summer, like making sundaes and sweet potato fries. Pretty soon I'm imagining that this is *our* kitchen, Becca's and mine, and that we're married and have a couple of kids, who are outside playing (wearing *lots* of sunblock), and the thought of being married to Becca makes my face go hot. I can tell my cheeks must be red, but Becca doesn't say anything, not like that time when she pointed at my face and said she wanted a cherry on top just that color. She doesn't even seem to notice.

I'm trying to figure out a way to ask her what it's like having a stepdad and was it hard for her to move away from where her real dad lived when her parents got divorced, and I think I'm almost ready when there's a knock on the kitchen door. Three knocks, followed by two knocks, followed by one.

Becca's face lights up. "That's Cody!" she goes, running to the door.

And in walks Mr. Perfect Teenage Boy, carrying an armful of Perfect Puppy-Pandas, who are squirming to get free.

"Ooh, the babies!" Becca squeals. Taking Max from Cody, she lifts him up to her face and buries her nose in his belly. "Ooh, who's my scrumpshee-umpshee!"

I expect Cody to give me a guy look that says, Girls! What're you gonna do? But he doesn't. He just nods in my direction like I'm the plumber who's come to fix a leak under the sink and says, "Hey, how's it goin'?"

Then, turning back to Becca, he goes, "Beck, you gotta see this. I taught Max and Charlie this cool trick. Here, sit down on the floor and put your legs out in front of you."

Beck?

And that's it. All of a sudden, we're right back in the Candy Kitchen the day Becca came in with Royal and Sara. It's like I don't exist. She's all eyes on the puppies . . . and Cody. I don't even get a text message under the counter. Everything the puppies do and everything that Cody says make her giggle. The one time I say something— something I personally think is pretty darn funny—she just smiles politely, like I'm the slightly-smarter-than-average plumber who's come to fix a leak under the sink and wasn't that clever and aren't I almost finished and ready to leave.

So I say, "Well, I better get going."

When I get nothing back, I say, "Don't forget to use your sunblock."

Becca looks up at me with this expression that says I really *am* a Cotton-Headed Ninny Muggins.

"So, I'll see ya," I go. "Thanks for the Diet Coke."

"No worries," Becca says, hardly looking up as Max leaps over her outstretched legs for, like, the tenth time, and I think, *No worries. Good luck with life, pal.*

Not Like It Was Going to Happen Anyway

It's out of the way, but I've got over an hour before I have to be back home to meet my dad. I still don't have any answers for him and where I'm headed probably won't give me any, but it's where I need to go. And even though it's hot, it feels good to be riding my bike. It reminds me of all the times after my dad left when I'd hop on my bike and hit the road, not knowing where I was going, just wanting to feel the wind fly by me as I went.

By the time I reach the shelter I'm so thirsty that even the thought of the warm water in the fountain just inside the door sounds good. But when I open the door, I forget all about my thirst and head straight for the front desk.

I'm in luck. That nice lady named Peg is there, and she remembers me.

At first she seems happy to see me, but then

her smile collapses in a way that tells me my luck just ran out.

"Are you here to see Licky?" she asks.

"Um, yeah," I go. "I mean, if it's okay."

"Oh, I'm so sorry," she says. "Licky was adopted yesterday."

"Yesterday?"

"I'm afraid so."

"Can you tell me who took her?" I ask, trying not to sound pitiful.

Shaking her head and giving me a look that says I am pitiful even if I'm trying not to be, she says, "I'm really sorry, honey, but I can't do that. We're not allowed to give out that information. I wasn't here yesterday, so I didn't meet the people who adopted her, but I'm sure she's found a good home. I know how much you liked her, and it's not the same, but would you like to look at some of the other dogs?"

I shrug and tell her no thanks.

"Well, maybe another day. You come back any-time. Okay?"

"Sure. Okay."

I walk back outside, past the fountain with its warm water, and get back on my bike. And now I'm heading home to go have lunch with my dad, who's going to try to convince me to leave the only place I've ever known and go live with him in a strange city two hundred miles away. And what I'm thinking is, what do I have to lose?

Top Ten Reasons

1. We can go bowling anytime we want.
2. It'll be easier on your mom. She'll have one less mouth to feed.
3. You won't have to work.
4. Gerri is way cool. She'll teach you how to play the electric guitar.
5. We'll get you your own electric guitar.
6. You can play in our band.
7. Hey, would your mom let you play in a band? No way.
8. A boy needs his dad, especially when he's a teenager.
9. If anybody busts your chops, I've got your back.
10. I miss my son.

The Rest of the Conversation

Burger King this time. I'm having a Double Stacker and my dad ordered a Triple Whopper. If Addie were here, she'd be lecturing both of us and we wouldn't hear the end of it until we dropped dead. And then she'd blame the burgers. In case you haven't guessed it: Addie's a vegetarian.

What I'd probably tell her is that we need meat to get through this conversation. Heavy amounts of meat.

"You got something that's mine," my dad says for openers.

"What're you talking about?"

"I think you know. Listen, you want a picture of me and Gerri so bad, all you got to do is ask."

I reach into my pocket and hand over the picture.

Putting it in his own pocket, my dad says, "Tell your mom thanks for letting me know. Did you take anything else she didn't find? Just curious."

I mumble no and keep my attention on my tray. BK fries are tasty, but not as good as Betty & Pauls curly fries or our sweet potato fries at the Candy Kitchen. Hey, maybe we should call it the CK.

"Anything else in the glove compartment interest you?"

I keep my head down and mumble.

"What'd you say?"

"I said, now that you mention it."

"Now that I mention it, what?"

Lifting my head, I say, "Now that you mention it, I did find something of interest. How come you didn't tell me the truck isn't even yours?"

"That all you got, Sherlock Holmes? Big deal. It's Gerri's. What's hers is mine; what's mine is hers."

"That go for the Beast, too?"

Now he's the one studying his tray, then the parking lot outside his window.

"I sold it. So?"

"So, what? You lied to me."

He turns his face to me. "Yeah, I said I still had

it. I wanted you to think that. That's the worst lie I ever tell, sue me. I sold it about a year ago, all right? I was strapped for cash. Gerri and me, we were already together then. She had the Ranger and this Honda Civic with some miles on it. That was enough cars for the two of us. And like I said, I needed the money."

This hits me hard. My dad's bike was always a part of who he was. A big part. Trying to imagine him without it, it's just one more way I don't get who he's become.

"So what's up with the tie?" I ask. "You throw out all your jackets when you sold the Beast?"

"You kidding me? I didn't throw out my jackets. Someday I'm going to have a bike again. The only reason I was wearing that stupid tie is because my lawyer said to. He said I should show up looking respectable so your mom would go along with the divorce. You want to know how long it took me to remember how to tie one of those things?"

"Not really."

"That's good," he says, "because talking about

it would be even more boring than trying to tie it."
That gets a smile out of both of us.

And this is when he goes into his top ten reasons
I should come live with him and Gerri. They're good
reasons, even if number three ("You won't have to
work") feels like he's laying a guilt trip, and number
five ("We'll get you your own electric guitar") is a
bribe. But it's the last three that really get to me:

"A boy needs his dad, especially when he's a
teenager."

"If anybody busts your chops, I've got your
back."

"I miss my son."

For over two years now, I've blamed my dad for
everything from making my mom and me have to
work so hard to global warming. I've cursed him
out and wished him dead. I've taken some of the
photos my mom took off the wall and burned them
in the bathroom sink. And the whole time I kept
wearing his jacket and slicking back my hair so I
could look like him. Because guess what? Dr. Leslie
was right. I wanted to bring him back.

And here he is, sitting across from me at BK, telling me he wants to bring *me* back, and what am I supposed to do? What am I supposed to say?

"How come you want me and not the girls?" I ask.

That throws him. "It's not that I don't want the girls," he says. "I love the girls as much as I love you. But Gerri and me, we're just getting started. I can't throw a whole big family at her all at once. And I wouldn't do that to your mom. And anyway, you were always my special guy. You know that, right?"

I nod, even though being his "special guy" is news to me.

"I want my boy back, my buddy, okay? That's all it is."

I keep nodding my head, like I get it when what I'm really thinking is, *I wish my friends were here to help me figure this out.*

"Can I have the weekend to think about it?" I go. "I need time to—"

"I know. You need time to sort it out. Look, I should have said something earlier in the week, but I had to run it by your mom first. The thing is, I've got to leave tomorrow. I want you to come with me. I wish I didn't have to go, but I've got work on Monday and there's this thing with Gerri's family on Sunday and . . . hey, you want to talk to her?"

"What do you mean? Now?"

"Yeah." My dad's reaching for his phone. "Talk to her, Skeezo. You guys are going to be best buds, I'm telling you."

"No, I don't think so, not now . . . I . . ."

Too late. The phone is ringing and it's in my hands.

"Hey, babe," says this sexy voice on the other end. My face goes redder than all ten letters in "Burger King."

"Um," I go.

"Whoa! Is this Skeezie?" She must be a genius, to have recognized me from one *um*.

"Yeah," I say. "So this must be, like, Gerri."

She lets out this big whoop of a laugh and right away I like her, this woman I'm picturing in a hot-pink sweater and big hoop earrings on the other end of the phone.

"I am *so* happy to meet you, Skeezie!" she goes. "I hope you're going to come live with us . . . oops, did your dad say something yet? Did I just screw this up?"

"No, it's okay. He said something."

"Well, good. Because if he hadn't, I *would.* Skeezie, you have *got* to come live with us, because I don't know how I'm going to get him to shut up talking about you all the time, if you don't."

I glance over at my dad, who's sitting there looking as happy as he does in that photo. He's grinning like an idiot, nodding his head at me, like, *See, isn't she great?* And I'm listening to Gerri go on about how great my dad says *I* am.

"You're his special guy," she says to me. "That's what he calls you." She keeps on talking—about being in the band and teaching me guitar, about how she's been cleaning out the spare room but waiting for me to get there to pick out the furniture, about all the fun stuff we're going to do together, about how much she loves to cook and how she hopes I like lasagna. I happen to love lasagna, but everything she's saying is just background noise to what I keep hearing in my head: *You're his special guy. That's what he calls you.*

I look over at my dad, with his eyes practically glowing and that idiot grin stuck on his face, and the answer is clear. I'm going.

There's just one question I have to ask him first. All I need is the nerve to ask it.

Skeezie's Super-Duper Franks 'n' Beans

By the time my mom gets home from work, I'm all packed. I started the minute I got home because I don't want time to change my mind. Jessie and Megan are parked in front of the TV where I stuck them a couple of hours ago with *Mulan II* and a bowl of popcorn. Glasses of water are set out on the table and supper's sitting on the stove: Skeezie's Super-Duper Franks 'n' Beans.

My mom's got an hour between jobs. There's part of me that's looking forward to telling her I'm going. *You wanted to kick me out? Well, you got your wish! Who's going to make supper now, huh? Who's going to be here when Jessie gets sick and Megan steals your makeup? Who you going to cry to every time you feel sorry for yourself?*

But there's another part of me that just wants to get out of here without anybody noticing, because as much as I hate saying it, I'm going to miss my mom. I'm going to miss Jessie's hugs around my legs. I might even miss Megan.

I know I still have to ask my dad the Big Question, but I already figure that whatever the answer is, I'm going to say okay, I forgive you, because that's how good this new life is already tasting to me. A lot better than franks 'n' beans or spaghetti with store-brand tomato sauce. Better than Becca making me feel like a loser. And Kevin humiliating me every chance he gets and me not having the guts to stand up to him. Better than feeling like a sap for falling in love with a dog I couldn't have even if she was still at the shelter. Even if she showed up on my doorstep with a big I'M YOURS sign around her neck.

Yeah, I know I'll miss my mom and my sisters and this dump of a house. I'll miss Steffi and the Candy Kitchen. And I'm seriously going to miss my friends. But hey, they still have each other. And they have families they do stuff with. Families that don't yell or cry or make them feel like all they're good for is the money they bring in and the supper they put on the table. But then there's the Forum and being Joe's earring brother and hanging out with Bobby and putting up with Addie.

Okay, I've got to stop thinking about this because I don't want to convince myself I'm making a mistake. I'm not. This is the best thing I've ever done. Someday I'm going to be in a band. Maybe we'll play Elvis covers. We could call ourselves Also Known as Elvis. That would be cool. It's like Joe always comes up with these other names for himself. JoDan. Scorpio. He's always, what do you call it, *reinventing* himself. Maybe that's me, too. I was Schuyler when I was born. My parents thought my nickname would be Sky, which would have been awesome. But somehow, nobody remembers how, I got tagged with Skeezie. And it stuck. And I've been Skeezie up until Steffi started calling me Elvis. And now who am I going to be? I'm going to be this kid who lives in Rochester, New York, with his dad and a stepmom who plays electric guitar and laughs like she's making music. As for the rest of it, who knows?

Maybe I'll be a guy that girls like and other guys respect. Anything's possible when you're reinventing yourself.

I hear my mom shout at Megan and Jessie to turn off the TV and come eat.

The TV clicks off midsong, but Jessie keeps singing, "'I wanna be like other girls'" at the top of her lungs, which makes Mom cry, "Jessie! You're on my last nerve!"

I shut my bedroom door behind me, not wanting anybody to see my packed bags yet, and go into the kitchen, expecting to find my mom in some kind of rage. But instead she's standing there putting a bunch of daisies in the middle of the table. She looks up at me when I come in and smiles. Actually smiles.

"I picked up this vase at a porch sale on the way home," she goes. "I thought it would be nice to have flowers for a change. Remember how we used to put flowers on the table every Friday night?" Meaning, *she* used to put flowers on the table.

I do remember. "I liked that," I tell her.

"Me, too," she says, then calls out, "Girls! Wash your hands and come to the table. I've got to leave in thirty minutes!"

She starts to tell me to wash my hands, too, then stops herself when I hold them up and she sees they're already clean. That's something else that's changed this summer. I used to be a total slob. But working at the Candy Kitchen, I had to clean up my act. I guess my friends were right. OMG, I'm wholesome!

While my sisters fight over the soap in the bathroom just feet away from where we're standing, my mom gets all misty-eyed and says in a soft voice so they won't hear, "I'm going to miss you, Skeezie."

"How do you know I'm goin' anywhere?"

"I just know," she says.

"Well, it's what you want, right? You're kicking me out, right?"

The mist turns to light rain, and she tears off a square of paper towel to wipe her eyes. "How can you say that?" she goes. "I just want what's best for you. You should be with your dad. It's selfish of me . . ."

She stops when the girls arrive at the table.

"What?" Megan says. "What are you two talking about?"

"Nothing," says my mom. "I'm just tired."

"You're always tired," Megan says, and I tell her, "Leave her alone. She works hard."

And we sit down at the table, nobody talking for the longest time, just Jessie humming "I Wanna Be Like Other Girls," between forkfuls of Skeezie's Super-Duper Franks 'n' Beans.

The Night Before the Longest Day

Friday night I hardly sleep.

Saturday is going to be the longest day I've ever had to get through. First, I have to mow Addie's lawn. It hits me that I'm going to have to tell her dad that I can't do it anymore. I don't think he'll care; he'll be glad to get his favorite form of meditation back.

Then I have a five-hour shift at the Candy Kitchen, although I figure what's the point, since I'm going to quit. Who knows, maybe Donny will kick me out and tell me he doesn't ever want to see my face in there again. And Steffi might say I'm letting her down when she was counting on me and she doesn't want to be my friend anymore. The thought of that makes me sick to my stomach, and one time during the night I have to run to the bathroom because of it.

And *then* I think how I have to tell my friends.

That's going to be the hardest part of the whole day. They all texted me—even Bobby, who said he and his dad were at a museum or something and he had two bars of power—to say they'd be getting home in the afternoon, and we came up with this plan to meet at four at the Candy Kitchen when I get off work. My dad's picking me up at the house at six, so I have less than *two hours* to say to my friends, "Welcome home! And by the way, I'm leaving forever."

Every once in a while I drift off to sleep. When I do, I have this same dream in which Addie and Joe and Bobby come home. They get all excited to see each other and act like I'm completely invisible.

The Skeezie-Steffi Dialogues: The Future

Steffi: You're sure?

Skeezie: Why wouldn't I be?

Steffi: You like it here, remember?

Skeezie: I'll come back and visit.

Steffi: It's not the same.

Skeezie: Look, maybe it won't work out and I'll move back here. Who knows? But right now . . .

Steffi: No, you're right. It's just . . . now I'm going to have to put together a whole new playlist. And who am I going to call Elvis?

Skeezie: What about your boyfriend?

Steffi: Alex? He's hardly the Elvis type. Besides, I broke up with him last night.

Skeezie: Why?

Steffi: Because I don't want to get married and have babies. Not yet. I've got another

	semester at community college and then I'm going to a four-year school and getting a degree.
Skeezie:	Around here?
Steffi:	Mm-mm. In Vermont. I'm going to a culinary institute.
Skeezie:	Say what?
Steffi:	Cooking school. I'm going to learn how to cook.
Skeezie:	You already know how to make every kind of ice cream dish and sweet potato fries. What else is there?
Steffi:	(laughing) Seriously.
Skeezie:	So you're leaving, too.
Steffi:	I guess. But I'll be back.
Skeezie:	Says you now.
Steffi:	Says me now. You're right. Who knows what the future will bring?
Skeezie:	The future's scary.
Steffi:	And exciting.
Skeezie:	So even if I stayed, you'd be going. And then who would call me Elvis?

Steffi:	I would leave strict instructions. Or make you a button: "Call Me Elvis." Hey, why didn't we think of that? This whole time you're wearing that ridiculous "Hello My Name Is Skeezie" badge, when it should say . . .
Skeezie:	Elvis. Right.
Steffi:	You're a nice kid, Big E.
Skeezie:	I told you, I'm calling you in five or six years. You said you'd marry me, remember?
Steffi:	I did?
Skeezie:	Ouch. Back in the fall, remember? I said I'd call you in five or six years and ask you to marry me.
Steffi:	Oh, right. You said you'd ask. I didn't say I'd say yes.
Skeezie:	Well, just in case, it's a good thing you broke it off with what's-his-name.
Steffi:	Alex.
Skeezie:	Yeah, but he's out of the running now. You're all mine.
Steffi:	You're trouble, you know that?

Skeezie: Nah. I just look like I am. Inside I'm a pussycat.

Steffi: I got news for you. You never had me fooled.

Skeezie: So you gonna marry me, Steffi? I know it's like your secret dream to be Mrs. Elvis.

Steffi: Uh-huh. Let's see what happens to you after a few years in Rochester. Grow up, come back, and we'll talk. But right now you'd better go talk to Donny. He's not going to be happy you're leaving.

Skeezie: I know. I'm sorry to give him such short notice.

Steffi: It's not that, you nitwit. He likes you. He's going to miss you because he likes you.

Skeezie: Yeah?

Steffi: Yeah. Now go talk to him before we get busy again.

Skeezie: Okay. Oh, and Steffi?

Steffi: Mm?

Skeezie: Three points to you for using "nitwit" in a sentence.

All the Friends Are Reunited

When I tell him, Donny gets a little miffed (one of Grandma Roseanne's words), but who can blame him? I'm leaving him shorthanded. Then he says, "You can have your job back anytime, kiddo. You're a hard worker and a quick learner. I should probably kick your butt for sticking me with Henry, but I want you to come back. So instead you can look for a little something extra in your last paycheck."

Three hours later I've got that paycheck in my hand. He's added on forty bucks. I can hardly believe it. I go into the kitchen to thank him, and when I come back out there are three people standing just inside the front door.

"Well, look what the cat dragged in!" I go.

"*Tous les amis sont réunis!*" Joe cries.

Translation in my head: "I'm here, I'm queer, get used to it!"

Actual translation: "All the friends are reunited!"

It's a few minutes to four. Addie, Joe, and Bobby are back.

"We all got you presents!" Bobby announces.

"Mine is the absolute best," says Addie, "if I do say so myself."

"Nuh-uh. Mine!" says Joe. He is wearing a T-shirt that reads HAPPILY MARRIED TO A CANADIAN in rainbow colors. I sincerely hope he did not get me one that matches.

"Mine is not very exciting," Bobby says apologetically, "but shopping options are limited in the woods."

"That only makes it more of a challenge," goes Joe. "Come on, Skeezie, open your presents. Oh, and I'll have a double hot fudge sundae with pistachio and mint chocolate chip. I'm in a green mood."

I go to make the sundae when Steffi says, "Sorry, fella, you're no longer employed here."

A glance at the clock tells me it's four. I untie my apron and hand it to Steffi. "I guess I have to pay like everybody else now, huh?" I say.

232

"I think the last Dr Pepper float is on the house," she says.

"And sweet potato fries?"

"Now you're pushing your luck. Go on, Big E, sit down. One Dr Pepper float and a jumbo order of sweet potato fries coming up!"

"Don't forget the double-green sundae!" Joe calls out.

After taking Bobby and Addie's orders, Steffi whispers in my ear, "Good luck telling them."

No kidding. They're sitting in the booth—*our* booth—with presents for me. Why'd they have to get me stinkin' presents? It's hard enough.

"What's up with the presents?" I ask, sliding in next to Addie.

"You're welcome," says Joe.

"We didn't plan it," Addie says. "We just all had the same idea."

"Yeah," says Joe. "It was just coincidental, so, so . . . *comment allez-vous.*"

"What?" Bobby asks.

"Okay, that means 'how are you,' but the point

is we all thought of it independently—and no, I have no idea how to say that in French."

"What Joe is trying to say in his limited *English* vocabulary," Addie says, "is that we all thought about you being stuck here, not having a vacation at *all* this summer, which is so *unjust*, and we all brought you a little something to cheer you up. Open mine first. No, wait, save the best for last. Joe, you go."

"Fine, fine, *quel chien*!"

Addie lets out an exasperated sigh. "That means 'what a dog.'"

"What. Ever. Here, Skeezie. Or Big Eyeballs, or whatever your name is."

Joe thrusts this big box at me that's all wrapped in paper with maple leaves on it. "Everything is authentic Canadian, eh?" he says.

"What?"

"Eh?"

"What?"

"That's what everybody says in Canada when they're not speaking French."

"Eh?"

"*Oui.* Eh."

"Know what I say to that?"

"Eh?"

"Meh."

Joe and I high-five, Bobby giggles, and Addie rolls her eyes. It's good to have my friends back home.

"There'd better be a moose inside," I tell Joe as I rip open the paper.

"Better than that," says Joe.

He's right. There are two moose—meese?—inside.

"These are way cool," I tell him, pulling out two ginormous moose slippers from the box. "But what size did you get? Twenty?"

"Twelve," he goes. "Come on, Skeezie, you have the biggest feet on the planet, outside the circus. If they're too big now, they'll fit you in a few years."

"Or you can use them to serve pancakes," Bobby says.

We all stare at him.

"I think you've been out in the woods too long," I say.

He brings up this small shopping bag from the seat next to him and slides it across the table. "Sorry it's not wrapped or anything," he says. "I think the store didn't even have wrapping paper."

"It's okay," I go. "Who cares about wrapping paper?"

From inside the bag I pull out pancake mix and a big bottle of maple syrup.

"I remembered how you told me that you and Megan and Jessie like pancakes and real maple syrup," he says. "I hope it's not a dopey present."

It's so *not* dopey that I'm having trouble saying anything. All I can think is how I'm not going to be there in the morning to make breakfast for my sisters. I'm going to be in some strange kitchen in a strange city. Who knows what they even eat in Rochester?

Finally, I manage to say, "Thanks, Bobby. This is the best present ever."

"Well, second best," goes Addie.

"Third best," says Joe.

Addie hands me a small wrapped rectangular box. I notice that the paper is covered with music notes and that Addie's hands are covered with graffiti.

"One," I say, "is it a harmonica? Two, why are your hands covered with graffiti?"

"One," she answers, "open it and find out. Two, this is not graffiti, O Ye of Little Culture. It's called *mehandi*. Or henna. It's like a temporary tattoo that's done in India. Only my grandma found this place near her that does it, so we didn't have to travel that far. Remember, I told you?"

"Oh, right," I say, recalling the *many* texts Addie sent me about what she and her grandma were up to. "Cool."

"Open it!" she says excitedly. "I have to be honest and tell you that Grandma picked it out."

Judging from Addie's face, there's something inside that I'm going to like—and there is. "An Elvis watch!" I go. "This is freakin' amazing!"

And like magic, "Blue Suede Shoes" comes up on the playlist. I can't resist. I strap on the watch, jump up, and start singing and air-guitaring, nearly crashing into Steffi, who's bringing our order. I take the tray, set it down on the table, and grab her hands. "Go, cat, go," I'm singing as Steffi and I start moving around the room.

It's the second time ever that I've danced with a girl.

For the next hour and a half, we're sitting there, me and the gang, catching up on their vacations. They keep asking me stuff about what's been going on here, but there's a lot I don't want to tell them.

I do tell them about looking at guitars with my dad. And I tell them about Becca. Right away Addie says, "See? Didn't I warn you? I *told* you to be careful. Becca is *so* fickle. One day she's your friend, the next day she acts, like, hello who are you. I mean, she's a lot better than she used to be, but she still wants to be popular, and that's a problem. *And* she is the biggest flirt! I'm sorry, Skeezie, she does like you, but who knows if that means as a friend or a boyfriend? Becca probably flirts with the mailman."

"And the toaster!" cries Joe.

"And her shoes!" says Bobby.

And we're off and running with a long list of things and people Becca flirts with. The whole time, part of me is laughing and happy and another part of me is worried sick.

Finally, when I look down at my new Elvis watch and see that it's five thirty, I say, "Guys, there's something I've got to tell you."

And the Winner of the Worst Person in the World Award Goes to . . .

Me.

And the Winner of the Worst Moment in My Entire Life Award goes to . . .

Now.

Nobody speaks. Joe is crying. Addie and Bobby look like they might cry, too.

"Do I have to give my presents back?" I say stupidly.

"That's not funny," says Addie, not understanding that I was being sincere, even if it was a stupid question.

"It's not like forever," I go. "I'll be back."

"When?" Bobby asks.

"To visit," I mumble.

Nobody says, "What? What did you say?" because nobody wants to hear.

"Why did you wait until the last few minutes to tell us?" Joe asks.

Now I'm going to start crying. I just shake my head and mumble, "Sorry, sorry, sorry."

The Rolling Stones are singing, "Time is on my side, yes it is," and I think, *What a joke*, when the only other sound I can hear is my Elvis watch ticking away the seconds.

"I've got to go," I finally say when the lump in my throat has gone away. "I like my presents a lot and I'm sorry I waited to tell you and I'll be back, I promise. I just need to be with my dad, I'm sorry. Hey, Joe, how do you say that in French?"

"*Au revoir*," says Joe, wiping his eyes with the back of his hand.

I'm no dummy. I know that doesn't mean "I'm sorry." It means "goodbye."

Even though we're all kind of in a state of shock, we manage to get up from the booth and give each other hugs. I think how this is the last time I'll sit in this booth with my friends. How the Gang of Five is no more.

Steffi gives me a hug, too, and even Donny comes out from the kitchen to hug me—one of those guy hugs, with slaps on the back.

As I'm going out the door, the Stones are singing, "You'll come running back, you'll come running back to me."

And that's when I totally lose it.

The Empty Place

I'm not the only one crying when I get home. Jessie is bawling her eyes out. She runs to meet me halfway up the sidewalk, throws her arms around my legs, and bellows, "Don't leave me!" so loud I figure at least one of the neighbors is sure to call the cops.

My mom comes out of the house, her face red and puffy. "I told the girls about an hour ago," she says. "I said you were going to be with your dad for a while."

I don't correct her. "For a while" is what Jessie needs to hear. And, to be honest, it's what I need to hear right about now, too.

"Where's Megan?" I ask.

"In her room," my mom says. "She's mad."

"That figures."

"Maybe you should go talk to her. Your dad called to say he's running late. He'll be here in about ten minutes."

Jessie clings to my legs as I go into the house, smearing my jeans with her tears and snot. "Wait'll you see the neat slippers Joe got me," I tell her. "Hey, look at my new watch."

"I don't care," Jessie says, sniffling. "I don't care about your watch."

When I get to the door of their bedroom, I lean down and tell Jessie, "I need to talk to Megan."

"Me, too," she says.

"No, I need to talk to Megan alone."

Jessie shakes her head angrily. "Me, too!" she says again.

I pull a couple of Candy Kitchen napkins out of my pocket and wipe her eyes and nose. "Okay," I tell her. I know a losing battle when I see one.

I knock on the door.

"Go away!" Megan shouts.

"Come on, Meggie," I say.

"Don't call me that, *Schuyler*!"

"Okay, fine, just let me in, okay?"

"Go *away*!" Megan repeats.

But there's no lock on the door, so I just push it

open. With Jessie attached to my leg, I enter their pink-and-purple room and sit down on the end of Megan's bed. She's huddled at the head, next to her pillows, hugging the Big Bird I won for her at the county fair when I was her age and she was five. It cost me almost all the money I'd saved up from my allowance to pop enough balloons in the water-gun race. But she wanted that Big Bird more than anything, and I wanted to be the one to win it for her.

"Look," I say, not sure what's coming next. "I need some time to be with Dad. A guy needs his dad, you know?"

"I guess I wouldn't know that, Skeezie," she says, practically hissing the words. "I'm a *girl*. I guess girls don't *need* their dads. Or dads don't need their girls, anyway."

"Okay, that was stupid. And he *does* need you. He just figures you belong here with Mom. You'll see, when you get older, when you're almost a teenager, you're going to see how important it is to have your mom to, you know, like, help you with girl stuff. Woman stuff. I need that kind of thing with Dad. I'm not saying I'm never coming back. I just have to do this right now."

I don't even know if I mean what I'm saying. It's just words coming out of my mouth.

"Fine," Megan says. "I know you don't like us anyway."

"What? That's crazy!"

"Well, you like Jessie. But you don't like me. You're always yelling at me."

Jessie clings to me even harder when she hears her name.

"You're always yelling at *me*," I tell Megan. "I like you just fine. It's just that we fight all the time."

Now Megan's eyes start welling up. "We don't have to," she says. "If you stay here, we don't have to fight."

"Oh, come on, Meggie," I say. "It's going to be okay. You've got Jessie and Mom. You don't need a stinky old brother like me around all the time."

"You're *not* a stinky old brother!" Jessie cries. "You're the best daddy ever!"

"What're you talkin' about? I'm not your daddy. I'm your big brother and you're going to be better off without me."

"Am not!" Jessie goes as Megan throws one of her pillows at me and says, barely above a whisper, "I hate you."

That's when I hear the horn honking and my mom knocking at the door, saying, "Skeezie, your dad's here."

My dad grabs the bags I've left piled at the front door. "I've got a surprise for you in the truck," he tells me.

I knew it. He got me the guitar. I want to tell him great. I want to be happy. But it's like the extra forty bucks in my paycheck, and the moose slippers, and the pancake mix and maple syrup, and the Elvis watch . . . none of them can take away the empty feeling I have inside. All these nice things people are giving me, they just make the empty place feel emptier. There's nothing that can change that. Not the Yamaha. Not even a Fender Strat.

I bend down to hug Jessie one more time, stand up to hug my mom. Megan is still in her bedroom, hiding out the way I did a couple of years ago in that crawl space under the house. I still haven't asked my dad the Big Question. I will, once we're on our way. But first I've got to go back into the house.

"I'll be right there," I tell my dad.

"Okay, but hurry up, 'cause you're going to like the surprise."

I find Megan still huddled on her bed with Big Bird.

I lean down and kiss the top of her head.

"I don't hate you," she whispers.

"I know you don't," I whisper back. "I don't hate you, either."

Minutes later, I'm walking down the sidewalk toward the Ranger, rehearsing in my head how I'm going to act excited about the electric guitar. But it's not a guitar that's waiting for me. There, looking out of the passenger-side window with a huge smile on her face, is Licky, full of dopey happiness and hope.

Halfway to Syracuse and Gerri's Making Lasagna

I feel like my heart is going to bust wide open. Licky hasn't stopped licking me from the time I got in the truck until about five minutes ago. Now she's curled up asleep on the blanket on the floor, my bare feet resting on her softly breathing belly. The empty feeling is gone; Licky jumped right in and filled it up.

"When are we going to be there?" I ask.

"What're you, four?" my dad goes. "You asked me that three times already, and we've only been on the road twenty minutes. We should be there by nine thirty, ten. Hey, Gerri's making lasagna for us. You like lasagna?"

"I love lasagna," I go. "Dad?"

"That's my name."

"Tell me again."

He sighs. "Man, you really are four."

"Aw, come on."

"Okay, okay. So you told me how much you loved this dog, right? And I said to myself, a boy needs a dog the way a boy needs his dad. That simple. I didn't know if you'd be comin' with me or not—this was Wednesday, remember, I hadn't even asked you yet—but one way or the other, I thought, 'Even if I get into big you-know-what with your mom, I'm getting us that dog.' So me and Del and Del's wife, Margie, went out to the shelter on Thursday and got her."

"And they had to be the ones to say they were adopting her, right?"

"Right. 'Cause, you know, I don't live here and they've got a fenced-in yard for their chickens and their dog Scooch."

"Did Licky and Scooch get along okay?" I ask.

"Oh yeah. Like gangbusters."

"Whatever that means."

"Well, let's just say that after two days they were best buddies."

"I hope Licky didn't feel sad leaving."

"Come on, Skeezo. They're dogs."

"I guess you're right."

We've got the windows open, with the breeze coming in warm and all, and Licky's belly is rising and falling under my feet. If I don't think back to the last couple of hours before I left, I'd have to say I never felt so, like, content. But then there's this thing nagging at me, this thing I feel like I've got to tell my dad.

"Does Scooch have to stay out in the yard?" I ask. "Like Penny did?"

My dad shakes his head and glances over at me, like he maybe knows what I'm getting at. "He lives in the house with them, but they let him out. He likes to chase the chickens."

"Will Licky live inside our house?"

"Oh, for sure."

"Is it okay with Gerri?"

"Are you kidding me? Gerri's nuts about the idea. She loves dogs. She had a dog when I first met her, but he was old and sick and she had to, you know . . ."

We both let it sit there, the knowledge of what she had to do.

"Dad," I go.

"Uh-huh?"

"When Penny ran away . . ."

"Yeah?"

"When she got out of her kennel . . . it was . . ."

I keep staring straight ahead as the road signs flash past, letting the rise and fall of Licky's breath hold me steady. "I know how she got out."

"You do?"

"Yeah, it was . . . it was me. I let her loose."

"What're you talking about, Skeezo? She got out in the middle of the night."

"I know. I couldn't sleep. I was worried about her. I worried about her every night. But that night, I don't know what it was, maybe I heard there was a storm coming or something, but I couldn't get to sleep. So I came up with this plan. I was going to sneak her into the house. Every night. I'd wait until everybody fell asleep, then I'd go out and get her and bring her in. And then I'd wake up first thing in the morning and sneak her back out.

"But it didn't work. Before I could get her leash on her, she took off. And we never saw her again."

I say this last part in a voice just above a mumble.

He answers in a voice about as quiet as mine.

"That's not entirely true," he says.

"Yeah, it is. I ought to know. I was the one who was there."

"No, I mean the part about never seeing her again. Since you're coming clean with me, I owe it to you to come clean, too."

With this, my dad pulls into a rest stop and cuts the engine. Licky wakes with a startled look, then seeing it's me, she licks my foot, lets out this snort, and goes back to sleep.

"Now listen, kid," my dad says. "I hope you won't be mad at me about this."

"Are you mad at me about letting her out?"

He shakes his head. "Hell, no. I don't blame you for that. You just wanted her inside the house where she belonged. You couldn't help it that she bolted."

"When she didn't come back, I was scared a car hit her or something."

"I know, but remember I told you that that didn't happen. I told you back then, remember? That I *knew* it didn't happen. I said I looked everywhere for her and that if she'd got hit by a car or something else bad had happened, we would have heard. It's a small town, Skeezie, right?"

"Right, but—"

"But the truth is, I found her."

My dad holds his eyes right on me. I don't know what to think. I'm doing a one-eighty from feeling content and happy to wanting to punch him right in his stupid face. How could he be telling me this seven years later?

"You found her?" I go. "You *found* her and you didn't tell me? You let me believe—"

"I *told* you I knew she was okay. I had to take her back to the pound, Skeezo."

"Don't call me that!"

"Come on, look, don't make this any harder than it already is. You told me your secret, I'm telling you mine. Your mom and me, we had Jessie on the way and I wasn't making diddly-squat at my job—whatever job it was then, who remembers—and your mom was seriously pissed that I went and got you a dog.

"After I found her, I just couldn't bring her back home, not if I was going to try to make things good again. Her getting loose, it just about broke my heart, for both of us—you and me—because we loved her so much. But it wasn't right for me to put my love of that dog on a higher shelf than my love of your mom. I had to make things good again. I had to try."

"So it's Mom's fault, is that what you're saying?"

"No. Man. Skeezie, it's nobody's fault. It's not your fault you let Penny out. It's not her fault she ran for the hills. It's not your mom's fault she couldn't handle having a dog with all else she had to deal with. And it's not my fault I was trying to be a grown-up and save my marriage."

"Well, you screwed that one up anyways," I say. "So what was the point?"

That punch I wanted to deliver? I just landed it.

My dad looks away and we sit there for a time, feeling the air between us grow thick.

Finally, my dad clears his throat and says, "How about cutting me some slack, huh? I'm trying. That's what this is all about. I got a good job, a good woman. After we get married, we're going to have a baby. I want you there with me, son. With us. I want you to be a big brother to whoever's comin' down the pike, you know? And meet my buddies and hang out, and be in the band. We're gonna have us some *fun*. Hey, wait'll you go fishing on this boat I was telling you about. It's a whole other thing from fishing back home. You're going to love it, I'm telling you."

"Okay," I mumble. "Whatever."

He starts the Ranger up and we drive for a long time, the radio playing, the sun getting lower on the horizon. Every once in a while Licky shifts her weight under my feet and lets out these little happy, contented sounds.

"Did she ever find another home?" I ask at one point.

"Oh, yeah," my dad says, knowing right away what I'm talking about. "I called to make sure. She was adopted the day after I dropped her off. They wouldn't tell me who, but they said it was a good home with lots of room for her to run around."

"And a house where she could sleep inside at night?"

"I didn't ask, but yeah. I figure."

I start to ask something else, but his hand darts to the radio and he pumps up the volume. "Check out this guitar riff," he says. "It's a thing of beauty."

My head is still full of what happened to Penny, full of what's happening to me, while his head is grooving to the music.

"Beautiful, right?" he calls out over the blasting music. "You're gonna play like that someday! We'll get you that Strat, and Gerri'll give you lessons. And what about this little brother or sister, huh?

Gerri's so psyched. I told her you're going to be an awesome big brother. Hey, she'll help you play guitar, you'll help her be a mom, right? Let's hope when the baby comes, it's a boy. These girls have got us outnumbered!"

That's when it all comes caving in on me. What am I doing in this truck? I don't want to be my dad's buddy or a member of his band. I don't want to help bring up his newest kid. I don't want to have *fun*. Well, I do want to have fun, but *my* fun, not his. I don't want to be the piece he slots into his life to make it perfect.

I want my dad, but not like this.

"I've got to go back," I mumble.

"What'd you say?" he shouts.

I reach over and turn off the radio and say in a loud, clear voice, "I've got to go back."

"You forget something?" he asks.

"No. Yes," I say. "I forgot my whole life. I want to be back home where I belong."

"We're halfway to Syracuse," he goes. "Gerri's making lasagna."

"Take me home," I say. "Dad, please."

"What about Licky? She's our dog, Skeezo."

"I thought she was mine," I say. "I thought you got her for me."

"I did, but . . . for us. For you and Gerri and me, for our family."

"I've already got a family," I tell him. "I want you and Gerri in it, too, but right now I want to go back to Mom and the girls."

"I'm going to have to take Licky with me," he goes. "You know that, right? Your mom will never let you keep her."

"Okay, all right, whatever. I'll see her when I come visit you and Gerri."

He looks over at me. "You're serious about this, aren't you?"

I nod.

"Will you come visit? Will you swear?"

I nod again.

"Gerri's going to cry, you know. She's been looking forward to—"

"Dad, stop. Please."

And so we turn around at the next exit and start the long trip back.

On the way we pull over for gas.

My dad tosses me his wallet. "I got a couple calls to make. Fill it up, son."

I'm standing here at the pump, not caring whether I look cool or not, just staring at the picture I found behind his credit card, the one of him and me and Jessie and Megan. It must have been about a year before he took off. We're out at the lake, sunburned from a day of swimming. We all look happy, even my dad.

Roses, of Course, and Lilies

It's eleven o'clock, closing in on the end of the longest day of my life.

Mom and I are sitting out on the front steps of our house. Up in the sky the stars are putting on a show.

"I can't remember a night like this," she says. "So black and the stars so bright. Of course, I'm usually in bed by now or still out at Stewart's."

"I wish you didn't have to work that job," I tell her. "I worry about you out there at night."

"You do?" She reaches over and rests her hand on my knee. "That's nice to hear."

"Maybe with me working, you could quit that job," I say.

"Maybe I'll just look for something else. Maybe there's something I can do from home, so I don't have to be away so much.

"Oh, look at that!" Her hand tightens a grip on

my knee. "A shooting star! It's early in the summer for shooting stars."

We gaze up at the sky, waiting for more.

It's been two hours since my dad and I pulled in. Mom and Megan and Jessie were all waiting for us when we did.

"Isn't it past your bedtime?" I asked Jessie.

"I'm too excited to sleep," she told me. "I *knew* you'd come back."

"You eaten?" my mom asked us.

"A bag of Doritos and half a bag of Twizzlers," I said.

"Healthy." Looking at my dad, she asked, "You want to stay for some supper? I can make eggs."

"No, but thanks," he said. "I need to get back on the road. I'll grab a slice of pizza or something."

I don't know what they talked about on the phone when my dad called from the gas station, but whatever it was had left them acting a whole lot nicer to each other. They had forgiveness in their voices, even if they didn't say the words.

When he left, my dad gave me a big hug—not the guy kind with slaps on the back, but the real deal—and I promised I'd come visit him and Gerri over winter break and stay for a week.

For supper I made pancakes with real maple syrup, which I heated up in the microwave. Jessie and Megan had a second supper with me. And I asked Bobby and his dad if they wanted to come over and join us. I didn't feel like talking much, so I asked them to tell us about their trip to the Adirondacks.

Bobby said, "We're going tent camping for a weekend in August. You want to come? Can he, Dad?"

Mike nodded his head. "You're welcome anytime, Skeezie. Think you can handle the bugs?"

"I can handle anything," I told him.

"Yeah, right," Megan said.

"He *can!*" said Jessie, grabbing my arm and covering it with about a thousand kisses.

"There's another one!" Mom says, pointing.

And sure enough a second star goes flying across the sky.

"That was nice of Bobby to ask you to go camping with them."

"Yeah, and nice of Mike to say he'd help you get your garden back. What kind of flowers will you plant? I don't even know what your favorites are."

"Well, roses, of course. I'm a romantic, like you. And zinnias and tulips. And lilies. I guess I'd have to say that lilies are my favorite."

Licky lifts her head from where she's lying at my feet and looks up at my mom with her happy, sad eyes.

"That's it!" I say. "We'll call her Lily! We can't keep calling her Licky. I mean, nothing personal, but that name is totally dumb."

If this were a movie or TV show, Lily would bark now and the camera would go in close on her big, smiling face while in the background you'd hear Mom and me laughing our dopey heads off. But in real life, Lily just yawns and goes back to sleep. And Mom and me, we just sit there thinking our thoughts until we're yawning, too.

"Lily's a good name for her," Mom says after a while. "She's a pretty dog."

"She ain't nothin' but a hound dog," I say. "And she's the sleepiest dog I ever did know. But she's a good dog. The best dog ever." I reach down and rub her head. "Thank you for letting me her keep her, Mom."

"Oh, you can thank your dad for that," she tells me. "He worked me upstream and downriver on the phone. He said you *had* to have that dog, that you *needed* that dog, that that dog and you were *meant* to be together. By the time he was done, I told him that one, he should be a salesman, and two, I had no doubt he was right."

"So you're where I get that whole list-making thing from," I say.

"You get a lot from me, buster, probably more than you'd like. But you get a lot from your dad, too. It's a good thing for you he's not *all* bad."

"Well, anyways, thanks for letting me keep her and letting her stay inside the house."

"Oh, you can thank your father for that, too."

"She won't be any trouble, I promise."

"Yeah, that's what they told me when you

were born, and look how that turned out."

I yawn and rest my head on her shoulder. "Skeezie," she says, "you have *got* to stop using so much mousse. It's disgusting."

"Okay," I mumble, without moving my head. "Can I unpack in the morning? I'll have time before I go to work."

"Sure," she says. "But you better let the dog out first, and don't forget to feed her. She's your responsibility."

"I can handle it. And her name is Lily."

"Fine. And I know you can handle it. If there's one thing in this world I am certain of, it's that you can handle it."

We sit there without moving for another six minutes. I know it's that long because I check the time on my Elvis watch. And then I get up, pull my mom to her feet, and call, "Lily! Come on, girl. It's time for bed."

FORUM: "The Importance of Fries"

Addie: I can't believe you're making me write this down. "French fries" is <u>not</u> an Important Topic.

Skeezie, Bobby, and Joe: What! Get real! Are you kidding!

Addie: Can somebody <u>please</u> tell me why I hang out with boys?

Skeezie: One, because you have excellent taste.

Bobby: Two, because boys know that "french fries" <u>is</u> an Important Topic.

Joe: Three, because boys are so darn cute.

Skeezie: And I repeat: You are so gay.

Joe: And you are so not. Although in that T-shirt . . .

Skeezie: I can't believe you're making me wear this. I am <u>not</u> "happily married to a Canadian!"

Joe: It's a present, Skeezie. Be nice.

also known as elvis

Skeezie: You said you got it for Zachary.

Joe: Yes, and he said it didn't fit. Which was his polite way of telling me he wouldn't be caught dead wearing it. So I regifted it to you.

Skeezie: Well, I'm wearing it until our food comes and then I'm taking it off.

Joe: Good idea. Just <u>thinking</u> about food, you get stains on your clothes.

Bobby: Speaking of which, where's your leather jacket?

Skeezie: At home. Duh. It's only, like, ninety degrees out there.

Addie: That never stopped you before.

Joe: You <u>always</u> wear your leather jacket.

Skeezie: Well, let's just say I'm giving it a rest.

Joe: <u>Mon dieu!</u> Don't tell us you're going to stop slicking back your hair!

Skeezie: No way. But I might use a little less mousse. Now can we get back on topic, please?

Joe: <u>Les pommes frites sont importantes!</u>

Skeezie: What does that mean? "The cat is in the bathtub"?

Joe: In fact, it actually means, the french fries are important. I have no idea how to say the cat is in the bathtub, and why are you thinking about cats in bathtubs? What's wrong with you?

Skeezie: I am not thinking about cats in bathtubs. I was just saying . . . oh, never mind! So, the important question of the day is which is better:
1. Betty & Pauls seasoned curly fries.
2. Burger King regular fries.
3. Candy Kitchen sweet potato fries.

Joe: Do we have to put our heads down on our desks when we vote?

Addie: No, this is an open and democratic forum, even if the topic is ridiculous.

Skeezie: Well, I vote for the sweet potato fries.

Joe: Of course you do.

Skeezie: Speaking of which, where are they?

Addie: Skeezie, if you start pounding on the
table . . .

Bobby: Or snapping your fingers.

Skeezie: I don't do that anymore. Get serious.

Bobby: Well, okay, if you want to get serious,
then I just want to say: I'm really glad
you're back, Skeezie.

Addie: Me, too. How could we be the Gang of
Five with only three people?

Joe: We were only four people, anyway. We
could have . . . oh, what am I saying?!
Skeezie, you are my earring brother! And
my writing partner! And <u>mon</u> best <u>ami!</u>

Skeezie: Really?

Joe: Well, <u>one</u> of my best friends. You and
Addie and Bobby. And Zachary. And . . .

Skeezie: Wow, thanks. Here, you can have your
shirt back.

Joe: No, wait! I was just going to say, and
your dog Lily-kins.

Skeezie: It's Lily. And thanks. But I'm still taking
off the shirt.

Addie, Joe, and Bobby:	Nooo!!!
Skeezie:	You guys. Re. Lax. I got another shirt on under it.
Bobby:	"Patsy Cline." Who's that?
Skeezie:	She's just the greatest country singer who ever lived.
Hellomy nameis Steffi:	See how smart he got while you guys were away?
Skeezie:	Thanks for the shirt, Steff.
Hellomy nameis Steffi:	You're welcome, Elvis. Okay, we got two orders of sweet potato fries, two regulars, and two seasoned curly fries.
Joe:	Wow, since when do you have curly fries?
Hellomy nameis Steffi:	Shh. They're from Betty & Pauls. And the regular fries are . . .

Skeezie: BK. Let the tasting begin!

Hellomy
nameis
Steffi: And then, Elvis, your break is over. You
            won't believe what Henry just did.

Skeezie: You don't have to tell me. I'll be right
            there, just as soon as these guys tell me
            that <u>our</u> fries are the best.

Bobby: Uh-oh. The ketchup bottle's empty.

Skeezie: Look at that. I'm not gone one day and
            the place falls apart.

Hellomy
nameis
Steffi: Where would we be without you, Elvis?

Skeezie: That's a good question. Let's talk
            about it after we finish these fries. Hey,
            Addie?

Addie: Yes?

Skeezie: You can stop writing now.

So that's the story, Elvis. I guess I should get used to calling you that. It's going to be your name, after all, even if it's my name, too. I hope your mom isn't planning on calling us Big E and Little E. That's cute for about five minutes. Like "Licky."

Speaking of whom, Lily is thirteen and a half now. She's in pretty good health, but dogs don't live forever. I sure hope she'll hang in there until you're big enough to get to know her. She's the best dog ever, and though you and I haven't even met yet, I just know you're going to be the best son ever.

And I'm going to try to be the best dad, even if I mess up, which believe me I will. One of the things I figured out the summer between seventh and eighth grade—the summer my dad came looking for me—was that being a dad came a lot easier to me than it did to him. I don't know what it was, maybe because I was kind of forced into the job at the age of ten—the man of the family, remember?—but I took to it like a natural. On the outside, I may have looked like a greaser, but that was just me trying to be like my father. The thing is, that wasn't really him, either. He was just trying to be something, too. Just trying to figure himself out, the way everybody does.

I got to know my dad a whole lot better in the years after that summer, and he got better at being a dad. I spent many weekends and vacations with him and Gerri and my half brothers. With the money I earned at the Candy Kitchen, I bought myself the Yamaha guitar at Strings 'n' Things. I took it with me on the bus every time I visited Rochester, and Gerri taught me to play. I'm pretty good. I'm even in a band now. It's kind of country-rock. We call ourselves the Sweet Taters. Three guesses how we came up with that.

A lot of things got better after that summer. My mom got a second job where she could work from home, and I kept working at the Candy Kitchen all the way through high school. I liked working there. Hey, I'm still working there! But I'll get to that in a minute.

In the fall, Bobby and his dad came over and helped my mom plant bulbs and plan her garden. My mom and Mike even dated for a while. It didn't work out, but they stayed really good friends, and it got both of them dating again. My mom's got this really nice guy in her life now. You'll meet him. His name is Rob. He's encouraging her to go to nursing school. I've got my fingers crossed that they'll get married, like Mike did a few years ago.

Addie and Joe and Bobby and I went into eighth grade and survived it. I didn't see much of Kevin Hennessey after that. He kept going to St. Andrew's, and he came into the Candy Kitchen once in a while, but mostly he drifted off and for the most part left me alone. I stopped worrying about him, anyway. I saw how, when you came right down to it, his life was kind of sad. I don't know what became of him.

As for Becca, well, she went back to the in-crowd. Her time hanging out with Addie and the rest of us was a blip on her path to popularity. That's what mattered most to her. She flirted and dated her way through high school, never landing for long with any one guy. But sometimes we'd see each other and smile, and those smiles of hers were like the secret texts she sent me that summer. They told me she still liked me and that she was sorry she couldn't be a better, more honest friend. Sometimes we'd even talk for a few minutes, and twice— or maybe three times—we got our dogs together to play. And then we talked and laughed like we really were friends. And that made me miss her all the times we weren't. But hey, she was just figuring herself out, too. I haven't seen her since high school. Maybe she's got herself figured out by now. I hope she's happy.

Bobby and Addie and Joe and me, we're still the best friends ever. Bobby's living in Washington, DC, working in politics at some job I don't understand. Addie is in Guatemala, building houses and teaching school. And Joe got married last summer. He and his husband live in New York City. They're all coming up here right after you're born. Even Addie, who said she'd swim all the way if she had to. And knowing Addie, she would. They can't wait to meet you, and anyway, they're your godparents, so they'd better show up, right?

As for Steffi and me, well, it's pretty funny how it all worked out—and lucky for you that it worked out at all! In the middle of eighth grade, while I kept working part-time at the Candy Kitchen, she moved to Vermont and went to this cooking school called the New England Culinary Institute. We kept in touch. I mean, we'd really become friends that summer—good friends—so even though we were so far apart in age, we could always talk to each other about the stuff that mattered. And as we grew older, the difference in our ages just wasn't that important.

But still, she was in college and I was in high school. And then she was trying to make a life for herself, working in restaurants in Vermont, and I was starting community college, not having a clue what I was going to do with my life. I hate admitting it, but I'm not much of a student. I'm no dummy, but I get bored easily, and restless. So I dropped out of college after a year, and that's when Donny asked me if I'd take over cooking at the Candy Kitchen and more or less run the place. Me, at nineteen, running the place! I liked it all right, but I enjoyed being out front more than in the kitchen.

So one day—I was twenty by then and your mom was twenty-six—I called her up and said, "Hey, Steff, why don't you come work for me? I need a cook." She thought I was joking, but she needed a job, so she said, "Sure, I'll help you out for a while."

Then I said, "Why not make it more than a while? Why don't you marry me as long as you're coming back?"

She laughed and said, "You need to grow up a little, Elvis. You still get food all over your face."

"I'm probably always going to get food all over my face," I told her. "Is that a reason not to love somebody?"

Well, she wasn't one to rush into things. She'd already been engaged once and broken it off. She came back to Paintbrush Falls and worked with me at the Candy Kitchen. She started adding really cool stuff to the menu, and the business grew. We brought back the jukebox and played the best music in town. We turned the place into such a success that Donny offered to sell it to us. I was twenty-one.

"We'll buy it," I told him. Your mom was standing right there next to me. "But on one condition. Steffi's got to marry me first."

Steffi turned to me, wiped the spaghetti sauce off my lips, and gave me a big kiss.

"Yes," she said. And we got married six months later. Your mom and me, we're good together. We always were, even when it was crazy to think about being anything more than friends.

So, Elvis, there are a lot of people waiting to meet you. Your mom and I are at the front of the line, of course, but you've got grandparents and aunts and uncles waiting, and Bobby and Addie and Joe. There are so many people waiting for you to be born. How great is that?

Oh, one last thing. I never did ask my dad the Big Question. I didn't need to, because I figured out the answer for myself—well, with your mom's help. She was right when she said he didn't come looking for me to say goodbye because it was too hard. But two years later he did come looking for me. And he found me.

Love,

Your dad, Skeezie

(also known as Elvis)

A Reading Group Guide
Also Known as Elvis
By James Howe

1. Does Skeezie's mom treat him more like a son or an adult partner?

2. Summarize Skeezie's relationship with Becca Wrightsman. What is their relationship like?

3. Would you say that Becca is a good person? How about Skeezie's dad? Why or why not?

4. The setting of *Also Known as Elvis* is in the small fictional town of Paintbrush Falls in Upstate New York. In the first book of the series, *The Misfits*, it's implied that Skeezie's leather-jacket-wearing, Harley-riding dad leaves this town because he doesn't fit in. But even though he slicks his hair back and wears his dad's old black leather jacket, Skeezie sees himself staying in Paintbrush Falls. Using

examples from the book, explain why Skeezie is comfortable in Paintbrush Falls and how he makes this small town his home.

5. Do any of Skeezie's friends need to leave Paintbrush Falls when they're older? Explain why.

6. Explain what Skeezie means by this simile/ extended metaphor: "I guess you could say I saw it coming, but it's kind of like hurricane warnings. You think, 'Yeah the rain's getting kind of heavy, but a hurricane? Not going to happen here. And then it hits. It had been raining pretty hard." What is happening in his family when Skeezie says this? Why does Skeezie use the image of the hurricane? Consider what happens before, during, and after a hurricane.

7. One of the themes in *Also Known as Elvis* is the effect of a father's abandonment on a family. Describe how losing her father affects Megan.

8. Though most of the novel is written in first person from Skeezie's point of view, the dialogue, forums, notes, texts, and "The Skeezie-Steffi Dialogues" give the reader added insights into the different sides of Skeezie. What do you learn about Skeezie from the other characters in the book?

9. Another theme in the novel is honesty and disclosure. Many characters in the story either lie or don't tell the entire truth. Skeezie says, "There were things I wasn't being honest about with my friends." What is Skeezie lying about? Are there other characters who are not open and honest? Find and describe points in the book where other characters lie.

10. In terms of the theme of dishonesty, explain why Licky/Lily and Penny, the dogs, are important in the book.

11. One aspect of great writing is using sensory detail. Skeezie spends a lot of time eating.

Make a list of at least ten different items that Skeezie eats, and write down the sensory details he uses to describe them.

12. Make a list of all of the different styles of writing used in the novel (e.g., song lyrics, lists, notes). What is your favorite style that was used, and why? How do these different styles contribute to Skeezie's story?

13. When Skeezie says that he is good at wisecracks, he is saying that he is funny. Find a comic scene in the novel. (There are many!) Analyze what makes the scene humorous. Are there literary devices used, like puns, hyperbole, or repetition, that add humor to the scene?

14. Many of the chapter titles are funny. Analyze them and explain what, if anything, makes them funny.

Guide written by Shari Conradson.
This guide, written in alignment with the Common Core Standards
(www.corestandards.org), has been provided by Simon & Schuster
for classroom, library, and reading group use. It may be reproduced
in its entirety or excerpted for these purposes.

ALL OF THE QUESTIONS.
ALL OF THE ANSWERS.

Judy Blume has a whole new look!
Which one will you read first?